"So why did you want me to come out to the barn?"

"I told you—"

"To brush down the horses at seven thirty in the evening," she said. "*Ya*, I heard you."

"Could be a guy just likes a little help with the work. Plus, I get a little restless, especially on winter nights."

She only smiled wider, and he knew that he wasn't fooling her.

He thought Rachel looked especially pretty in the glow of the lantern. He was suddenly glad that she had fallen into their lives. He was already starting to think of events in terms of before Rachel or after Rachel, as if she was some sort of dividing line in his life. She was certainly unlike any of the girls he had stepped out with.

What did that mean?

Was he falling for her?

It wasn't like she was staying here. It wasn't like they had a chance to build a life together. Then again, how much control did one have over who they fell in love with?

Vannetta Chapman has published over one hundred articles in Christian family magazines, receiving over two dozen awards from Romance Writers of America chapter groups. She discovered her love for the Amish while researching her grandfather's birthplace of Albion, Pennsylvania. Her first novel, *A Simple Amish Christmas*, quickly became a bestseller. Chapman lives in the Texas Hill Country with her husband.

Books by Vannetta Chapman

Love Inspired

Indiana Amish Brides

A Widow's Hope
Amish Christmas Memories

Amish Christmas Memories

Vannetta Chapman

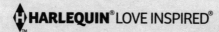

Recycling programs for this product may not exist in your area.

LOVE INSPIRED BOOKS

ISBN-13: 978-1-335-50988-8

Amish Christmas Memories

www.Harlequin.com

Printed in U.S.A.

And be ye kind one to another, tenderhearted, forgiving one another, even as God for Christ's sake hath forgiven you.
—*Ephesians* 4:32

He healeth the broken in heart, and bindeth up their wounds.
—*Psalms* 147:3

This book is dedicated to Vicki Sewell,
who is so much like family that she is family.
I know you know—but I love you.

Acknowledgments

I would like to thank my editor,
Melissa Endlich, for pushing me to write better.
I'd also like to thank the art department and
editorial team for helping me through the art
forms, line edits and everything in between.
Finally, thank you to my agent, Steve Laube,
for your continued guidance.

Also a big thanks to my family, who remind me
to step away from the computer and experience
this thing we call life. It's when I'm with you
that I find the heart of my stories.

And finally, "Giving thanks always for all things
unto God and the Father in the name of
our Lord Jesus Christ" (*Ephesians* 5:20).

Chapter One

Caleb Wittmer glanced up from the fence he was mending. Something had caught his eye—a bright blue against the snow-covered fields that stretched in every direction. There it was again, to the north and west, coming along the dirt road.

He stepped closer to the fence. His horse moved with him, nudged his hand.

"Hold on, Stormy." Caleb squinted his eyes and peered toward the northwest, and then he knew what he was seeing—he just couldn't make sense of it. Why would a woman be walking on a cold December morning with no coat on?

Goose bumps peppered the skin at the back of his neck. As he watched, the woman wandered to the right of the road and then back to the left.

Something wasn't right.

He murmured for the gelding to stay, climbed the fence and strode toward her. He'd covered only half of the distance when he noticed that she was wearing Amish clothing, though not their traditional style or color. She was a stranger, then, from a different community. But what was she doing out in the cold with no coat? More disturbing than that, she wore no covering on her head. All Amish women covered their hair when outside—Swiss, Old Order, New Order. It was one of the many things they had in common. The coverings might be styled differently, but always a woman's head was covered.

He was within thirty feet when he noticed that her long hair was a golden brown, wavy and thick, and unbraided.

At twenty feet he could see the confused look on her face and that she was holding a book.

At ten feet she tumbled to the ground.

Caleb broke into a sprint, covering the last distance in seconds. The mysterious woman was lying in the snow, her eyes closed. Dark brown lashes brushed against skin that still held a slight tan from winter. Freckles dotted the tops of her cheeks and the bridge of her nose. A small book had fallen out of her hands. Her hair was splayed around her head like a cloak she'd thrown on the ground, and a pale blue scarf was wrapped around her neck—but no coat.

Where was the woman's coat?

He shook her gently, but there was no response.

Looking up, he saw Stormy waiting for him at the property line. He'd never be able to take her that way, unless he was willing to dump her over the fence. He couldn't begin to guess why she had fainted, but throwing her over barbed wire and onto the ground wouldn't be helpful.

No, he'd have to go the long way, by the road.

Caleb shook her shoulders one more time, but still there was no response. He clutched her hand. Her fingers were like slivers of ice. How long had she been outside? Why was she wandering down their road?

Scooping her up, he turned toward the house.

She weighed little more than a large sack of feed, which he'd been lifting since he was a teenager. Carrying her was not a problem, but now his heart was racing and his breath came out in quick gasps. What if he was too late? What if she was dying?

He strode toward his parents' house, pulling her body closer to his, willing his heat to warm her, whispering for *Gotte*'s help.

Stormy kept pace on his side of the fence.

The farmhouse seemed to taunt him, as it receded in the distance, but, of course, that was impossible. It was only that he was scared now, worried that he should have seen her sooner, that he might be too late.

Snow began to fall in earnest, but he barely noticed. Tucking his chin to keep the snow out of his eyes, he increased his pace.

"She just collapsed?" His mother had taken the sight of him carrying a nearly frozen woman into their home in stride. She'd told him to place her on the couch as she'd grabbed a blanket.

"*Ya.* She teetered back and forth across the road and then fell into the snow as I was watching."

"No idea who she is?"

"Obviously she's not from here."

Ida nodded. Her dress was of a bright blue fabric, while their community still wore only muted blues and greens, blacks and browns. They were a conservative Amish community, a mixture of Swiss and Pennsylvania Dutch, which was why they lived in the southwestern part of Indiana. They weren't a tourist destination like Shipshewana. And unlike some more liberal Amish communities, they didn't abide solar panels and cell phones and *Englisch* clothing. Not that the woman's dress was *Englisch*. It was obviously plain in style, but that color…

He didn't normally notice the color of a girl's dress, but in this case…well, the blue fabric seemed obscenely bright. She remained unconscious, though she seemed to be breathing. Caleb pulled off his knit cap, shrugged out of his coat and tugged off his gloves. Squatting in front of the couch, he watched his mother as she attempted to revive the woman.

She murmured slightly, tossing her head left and right. Almost of its own volition, his hand reached out and touched her face. Her skin felt like satin.

Still she didn't wake.

"She had nothing with her?"

"Nein."

"No purse or coat or—"

Caleb jumped up, snapping his fingers. "A book. She was holding a book when I first saw her."

"You best go and get it. Perhaps her name is written inside. Maybe there's someone we can contact."

Caleb snagged his coat from the floor where he'd dropped it and hurried back outside. Fat snowflakes were still falling. It looked as if the current snowfall was going to be a significant accumulation for only the third of December. Already the front path was completely obscured, any trace of his previous trek across the yard erased. At this rate they would have a Christmas to remember. It was unusual, as most of their snow usually came in January.

He jogged back the half mile, passing the place where he had been mending the fence. His tools were still there. He'd need to return them to the barn, but that wasn't an emergency. The woman? She was. He slowed when he reached the tall pine tree and scanned the ground. Nothing, not even his footprints from earlier.

He'd forgotten his hat and the snow was cold and heavy on his head. He shook the snow off his head, wiped his eyes and walked up and down the fence line—a hundred feet in both directions. There was nothing, but he was sure that she had been holding a book of some sort. He closed his eyes, saw it fall from her hand as she dropped to the ground. She'd wandered off the east side of the road, closer to the fence.

This was not the way his Monday was supposed to go. He didn't mind helping a neighbor, or a stranger, but he'd had an entire list of chores to complete. Farm life, his life, worked better when he stayed focused on the things he'd committed to doing. *When women entered his life, trouble often followed.* He pushed that thought away as soon as it formed. This wasn't about him. He needed to find the book. He hadn't opened his eyes that morning knowing he would save a stranger from freezing to death, but now that he had there was nothing left to do but see this thing through.

They'd find out who she was and where she belonged.

They'd return her, and he could get on with his life.

But first he needed to find the book.

He turned east, walked back and forth between the road and the fence, making a zigzag type of pattern. Then just when he was beginning to think he'd imagined the entire thing, that he'd return home and find there was no mysterious woman on their couch, he spied it—a lump of snow where there should have been flat ground.

He dropped to his knees and brushed the snow away.

The book had a green-and-gold cover with a photograph of a snowy path going through the woods, and beneath that the words *The Road Not Taken and Other Poems*. Had he read something like that in school? He was twenty-five now and that had been many years ago. He shook his head, picked up the book and hurried back home.

When he walked back into the living room, his father was there, and his mother was placing a cup of hot tea into the woman's hands. She was sitting up now, looking around with a dazed sort of expression.

"I think this is yours." Caleb placed the book on the couch beside her.

"Danki."

That one word confirmed what he'd suspected earlier. She wasn't from their part of the state. The Daviess County Amish had a distinctive Southern twang. This woman didn't.

Caleb's father sat in the reading chair. His mother perched on the edge of the rocker. Caleb folded his arms and stood behind them both. Across from them, the woman stared at the tea, then raised her eyes first to his *mamm*, then his *dat*, and finally settled her gaze on him.

"What happened? Where am I?"

"You don't know?" Caleb glanced at his parents, who seemed content to let him carry the conversation. "You were walking down the road, and then you collapsed."

"Why would I do such a thing?"

Caleb shrugged. "What's your name?"

The woman's eyes widened and her hand shook so that she could barely hold the mug of tea without spilling it. She set it carefully on the coffee table. "I don't—I don't know my name."

"My name is John Wittmer," Caleb's father said. "This my *fraa*, Ida, and you've met Caleb."

"How can you not know your own name?" Caleb asked. "Do you know where you live?"

"Nein."

"What were you doing out there?"

"Out where?"

"Where's your coat and your *kapp*?"

"Caleb, now's not the time to interrogate the poor girl." Ida stood and moved beside her on the couch. She picked up the small book of poetry. "You were carrying this, when Caleb found you. Do you remember it?"

"I don't. This was mine?"

"Found it in the snow," Caleb said. "Right beside where you collapsed."

"So it must be mine."

"Perhaps there's something written on the inside." Ida tapped the cover. "Maybe you should look."

Caleb noticed that the woman's hands trembled as she opened the cover and stared down at the first page. With one finger, she traced the handwriting there.

"Rachel. I think my name is Rachel."

Rachel let her fingers brush over the word again and again. *Rachel.* Yes, that was her name. She was sure of it. She remembered writing it in the front of the book—she'd used a pen that her *mamm* had given her.

She could almost picture herself, somewhere else. She could almost see her mother.

"My *mamm* gave me the pen and the book...for my birthday, I think. I wrote my name—wrote it right here."

"Your *mamm*. So you remember her?"

"Praise be to *Gotte*," John said, a smile spreading across his face.

"Is there someone we can call? If you remember the name of your bishop..." Caleb had sat down in the rocker his mother had vacated and was staring at her intensely.

They all were.

She closed her eyes, hoping to feel the memory again. She tried to see the room or the house or the people, but the image had receded as quickly as it had come, leaving her with a pulsing headache.

She struggled to keep the feelings of panic at bay. Her heart was hammering, and her hands were shaking, and she could barely make sense of the questions they were pelting at her.

Who were these people?

Where was she?

Who was she?

She needed to remember what had happened.

She needed to go home.

Instead she dropped the book into Ida's lap and covered her face with her hands. "I think—I think I'm going to be sick."

She bounded off the couch and dashed to the kitchen, making it to the sink just in time to lose whatever she'd eaten. Unfortunately, the sink had been full of breakfast dishes. She turned on the tap and attempted to rinse off a plate, but her hands were shaking so badly that she kept knocking it against the side of the sink.

"I'll take care of that." Ida's hands slid over hers, taking the plate and setting it back into the sink. She pulled a clean dish towel from a drawer and handed it to her. "Come and sit down."

She sank into a chair at the table and pressed her fingertips to her forehead. If only the pounding would stop, she could think.

"We best take her to town," John said.

"I'll get the buggy." Caleb brushed past her.

She remembered being in his arms, the way he'd pulled her close to his body, the way he'd petitioned *Gotte* to help them. Or had she dreamed that? But then he turned, and his blue eyes met hers, and she knew she hadn't imagined it. She could smell the snow on his coat, remember the rough texture of the fabric, hear the concern in his voice.

"We best wrap her in a blanket," Ida said. "And bring the book. There might be other clues in it."

And then they were bundling her up and helping her into the buggy. The ride passed in a blur of unrecognizable farms and stores and hillsides. The only thing familiar was the clip-clop of the horse's hooves and the feel of the small heater blowing from the front of the buggy.

Had she been in a buggy just like it before?

Caleb directed the horse under a covered drop-off area, next to a door marked Emergency.

"I don't think—"

"That it's an emergency? *Ya*, it is." He helped her from the buggy. Ida had rushed in ahead of them, and John said he'd park the buggy and meet them inside.

The next few hours passed in a flurry of hospital forms and medical personnel and tests. Finally, the doctor who had first examined her walked into the room, computer tablet in hand. She was a young woman, probably in her thirties, with dark black hair, glasses and a quick smile. Something about her manner put Rachel at ease, though another part of her dreaded hearing what the woman was about to say.

John had left to find them coffee and a snack, but Ida and Caleb both stood when the doctor walked into the room.

"Thank you all for your patience." She motioned for them to sit back down. "I know the barrage of tests we put a patient through can be trying, but trust me when I say that it's important for us to collect as much information as we can."

She turned toward Rachel.

"Hi, Rachel. Do you remember me?"

"*Ya.* You're Dr. Gold."

"Great. Can you tell me what day it is?"

Her eyes darted to the whiteboard that listed the name of her nurse and orderly. "December third."

"Very good." Dr. Gold laughed. "We know you can read."

The doctor placed her tablet on the table next to Rachel's bed. "Mind if I check that bump on your head one more time?"

Rachel leaned forward and jerked only slightly when the doctor gently probed the back of her head.

"Still tender."

"*Ya.*"

"Still no memory of what happened before Caleb found you?"

"Nein."

"And you can't remember how you got this bump?"

"The first thing I remember is…is Caleb carrying me to his house."

The doctor plumped the pillows behind her, waited until Rachel had sat back and then shone the penlight in her eyes again.

"I'm sorry. I know this is uncomfortable."

"It's just the headache…"

Dr. Gold nodded in sympathy and then clicked off the light. "Rachel, you have a slight concussion, which is why you're experiencing a sensitivity to light, a blinding headache and nausea."

She remembered vomiting in Ida's sink and grimaced.

"How long will that last?"

"In most cases, symptoms improve in seven to ten days."

"That's *gut*."

"But the actual healing of your brain could take months."

"I don't understand."

"Most often a concussion occurs when you've sustained a blow to the head. In this case, you have a sizable knot at the back of your head and toward the top. Can you remember anything at all that led up to your accident?"

Rachel shook her head and spikes of pain brought tears to her eyes.

"I'm not surprised. You have what we call retrograde amnesia caused by a concussion. Often in such a situation, patients have problems remembering events leading up to an accident."

"I still don't understand."

"Retrograde amnesia or a concussion?"

"Both."

Dr. Gold smiled and patted her hand. "Concussions happen all too often. The brain itself is rather like Jell-O. When a concussion occurs, your brain slides back and forth and bumps up against the walls of your skull. Basically the brain is bruised, and like all bruises it takes time to heal."

"What would cause such a thing?" Caleb asked. His expression had turned rather fierce. "Does it mean that someone hit her?"

"Not necessarily." Dr. Gold cocked her head, studying both Ida and Caleb for a few seconds. Then she turned her attention back to Rachel. "You could have been in a car accident, or fallen off a bicycle or simply tripped, and hit your head against the ground."

"And that would cause a concussion?" Ida asked. "Just falling?"

Caleb sank back into the chair and leaned forward, elbows on his knees, fingers interlaced. "Did it happen when she fell in the snow?"

"Not likely," Dr. Gold said. "I suspect that Rachel sustained her injury before you ever saw her. It's why she was meandering back and forth across the road. Concussions often result in vertigo."

"Can you tell how long it's been?" Ida asked.

"I can't. There was no bleeding from the wound, so I rather doubt that someone hit her. More likely it was a simple accident."

"What about my memory?" Rachel asked. "When will it return?"

"Memories are tricky things. You remembered my name, and you know who these people are. Correct?"

"Caleb." She met his gaze, remembered again being in his arms. "And Ida, his *mamm*."

"Which is a good sign. This tells us your brain is still working the way it should."

"But I wouldn't have remembered my name if it hadn't been written in that book, and I still don't know where I live or who I am."

"In most cases those memories will return in time."

"How much time?"

"Remember what I said earlier? You don't just have a concussion. You also have retrograde amnesia."

"And what does that mean?"

"That it may be a few days or weeks or even months before you regain your memories."

Rachel felt as if she was falling into a long, dark tunnel. She stared down at the cotton blanket covering her and grasped it between both of her hands. "That long?"

"I'm afraid so, but the good news is that your memory is working now, and it will continue to work. You may not be able to remember what happened before the accident, but you can create new memories. Plus you're healthy in every other way."

"But what am I to do? Where will I live?"

"If you'd like, we have a social worker here at the hospital that can meet with you and find temporary housing for you. We'll also put you in contact with a liaison with the Daviess County Sheriff's Office. Perhaps your family has reported you missing. It could be that they're looking for you even now."

"What do I do until they find me?"

"Be patient. Give your brain time to heal. Live your life."

"I don't have any money, though."

"There are charities that provide funds for those in need. You don't need to worry about money right now."

"She doesn't need to worry about where to live, either." Ida stood and moved to the side of the bed. She was about Rachel's height but looked a bit shorter, owing to her weight. She wasn't big exactly, but rounded, like a grandmother should be. She was probably close to fifty with gray and brown strands of hair peeking out from under her prayer *kapp*. "Rachel, we would be happy to have you stay with us. We have an extra room. It's only Caleb and John and myself, so it's a fairly quiet environment. You can rest and heal."

Rachel didn't know if that was a good idea. Ida and John seemed like a nice couple, and Caleb had saved her, but she wasn't sure they wanted a brain-injured person living with them. Then again, what choice did she have?

She didn't want to go to a police station.

She didn't want to wait on a social worker.

"Stay with us," Ida repeated.

"Ya." Rachel nodded, wiping away the tears that had begun to slide down her cheeks. "Okay. *Danki.*"

Dr. Gold was pleased with the arrangement, and Ida was grinning as if Christmas had come early, but when Rachel glanced at Caleb, she wasn't sure if she saw relief or regret in his eyes.

Chapter Two

They returned to Ida and John's house. The snow had stopped, but it sat in heaps on the side of the road. The clouds had cleared, the sun was shining and Rachel suspected the snow would melt completely by the next day. The *Englisch* homes they passed already had Christmas decorations out on the lawn. Rachel wasn't sure what Amish homes did to celebrate for the season. She wasn't sure what her family had done in the past.

The rest of the day passed in a blur.

She met with the local bishop, Amos Hilty, a kind, elderly man as round as he was tall with tufts of white hair that reminded her of a cotton ball.

She learned that the local community was a blend of Swiss Amish and Pennsylvania Dutch Amish, but she couldn't tell them which she had been. From the style and color of her dress, they guessed that she came from one of the more progressive districts. Amos assured her that he'd contact the local districts to see if anyone had reported a young woman missing.

"We'll find your family, Rachel. Try not to worry. Trust that *Gotte* has a plan and a purpose for your life."

She wasn't sure how *Gotte* could use her accident, her loss of memory, for His good, but she smiled and thanked the bishop for helping her.

Several times that afternoon she had to excuse herself and lie down because of the vertigo and nausea, and bone-deep exhaustion. Ida's cooking smelled wonderful—it was a meat loaf she'd thrown together and served with mashed potatoes, canned squash, gravy and fresh bread. Rachel thought she could eat three plates, but when she'd taken her first bite, the nausea had returned, and she'd fled to the bathroom.

Now it was ten thirty in the evening and everyone was asleep, but she was starving. Pulling on the robe Ida had loaned her, she padded down the hall to the kitchen. She pulled a pitcher of milk from the icebox and found a tin of cookies when Caleb walked in.

"If you'd eaten your dinner, you wouldn't be so hungry late at night." When she didn't answer and just stood there frozen, as if she'd been caught stealing, he'd walked closer, bumped his shoulder against hers and said, "I'm kidding. Pour me a glass?"

So she did, and they sat down at the table together. She could just make out his outline from the light of the full moon slanting through the window. Oddly, the darkness comforted her, knowing he couldn't see her well, either. She felt less exposed, less vulnerable.

"I can't remember if I thanked you…for finding me in the snow. For bringing me here."

"You didn't."

"Danki."

"Gem Gschehne."

The words slipped effortlessly between them and

brought her a small measure of comfort. At least she remembered how to be polite. Surely that was something.

"You owe me, you know."

Her head snapped up, and she peered at him through the darkness.

"You scared at least a year off my life when I saw you out there."

"Lucky for me you did."

"I'm not sure luck had anything to do with it. *Gotte* was watching over you, for sure and certain."

"If He was watching over me, why did this happen? Why can't I remember anything? What am I supposed to do next?"

"I'm not going to pretend I have the answers to any of those questions."

"Might be a good time to lie to me and say you do."

Caleb's laugh was soft and low and genuine. "We both would regret that later."

"I suppose." She sipped the cold milk. At least her stomach didn't reject it. Maybe she would feel better if she could keep some food down. She hesitantly reached for an oatmeal cranberry cookie.

"Your *mamm*'s a *gut* cook."

"*Ya*, she is."

"So it's just you? You're an only child?"

"*Ya*, though my *mamm* wanted to have more children."

"Why didn't she?"

"Something went wrong when she had me, and the doctors said she wouldn't be able to conceive again."

"Gotte's wille."

"She always wanted a girl, too, so I suppose you're an answer to that prayer, even if you're a temporary answer."

"When you marry, she'll have a daughter-in-law."

"So they keep reminding me." He laughed again, but there was something sad and bitter at the same time in it. His next words had a serious, let's-get-down-to-business tone. "How are you feeling? I know you keep telling my parents that you're fine, but it's obvious you aren't."

"Lost. Confused. Sick to my stomach."

"Food should help settle your stomach."

She bit into the cookie, which was delicious but could use a little nutmeg. "I just remembered something."

"You did?"

"Cookies need nutmeg."

Caleb reached for another. "It's a beginning."

"Not much of one."

"The doctor told you this could take a while."

"I know…but can you imagine what it's like for me? I don't know who I am."

"You know your name is Rachel."

"Only because you found my book."

"Not many Amish girls read Robert Frost. That narrows the prospective field of candidates down a little."

"Perhaps we could advertise somewhere…"

"The Budget." Caleb nodded and ran a thumb under his suspenders. "Actually that's not a bad idea. If you write something up in the morning—"

"What would I write? I don't remember anything."

"Okay. *Gut* point, but perhaps your family will post there. We'll watch the paper closely."

"Danki."

"Gem Gschehne."

And there it was again—an odd familiarity that bound them together.

"Are you always this nice?"

"*Nein*. I'm on my best behavior with you because you've had a brain injury."

"Oh, is that so?"

"My normal personality is bullheaded and old-fashioned, which are both apparently bad things. And that's a direct quote."

"From?"

"My last girlfriend."

"Oh. Well, I can't remember my last boyfriend, so you're still a step ahead of me."

Caleb cleared his throat, returned the pitcher of milk to the refrigerator and then sat down across from her again. When he clasped his hands together, she knew she wasn't going to like what he was about to say. She suddenly felt defensive and bristly, like a cat rubbed the wrong way.

"My parents wanted to give you a few days to adjust, but I think there are some things you should know."

"There are?"

"Our community is quite conservative—we're a branch of the Swiss Amish, as Bishop Amos explained."

"He's a nice man."

"As long as you're staying...well, this is awkward, but..."

"Just spit it out, Caleb." She'd had this sort of conversation before, though she couldn't remember the details. Somewhere in her injured brain was the memory of someone else trying to set her straight. Why did people always think they knew what was best for her?

"Our women always keep their heads covered—always."

"Oh." Rachel's hand went to her hair, which was un-braided and not covered. "Even in the house?"

Caleb glanced at her and then away. Finally, he shrugged and said, "Depends, but my point is that for some reason you weren't wearing a *kapp* when I found you."

"Maybe I lost it."

"And your hair was down—you know, unbraided, like it is now."

She pulled her hair over her right shoulder, nervously running her fingers through it. "Anything else?"

"Your clothes are all wrong."

"Excuse me?"

"Wrong color, wrong...pattern or whatever you call it."

"The color is wrong?"

"We only wear muted colors—no bright greens or blues."

"Because?"

"Because it draws attention and we're called to a life of humility and selflessness."

Rachel jumped up, walked to the sink and rinsed out her cup. When she had her temper under control, or thought she did, she turned back to him. "Any other words of wisdom?"

Caleb was now standing, too, but near the table with his arms crossed in front, as if he was afraid she'd come too close. "Not that I know of...not now..."

"But?"

"Look, Rachel. I'm not being rude or mean. These are things I think you'd be better hearing from me than having people say behind your back."

"Is that what type of community you have? One that talks behind people's backs?"

"Every community does that, and it's more from curiosity and boredom than meanness."

"All right, then, tell me. What else do I need to know? So I won't incite gossip and all."

"It's only that you're obviously from a more progressive district."

"Oh, it's obvious, is it?"

"And so you might want to question your first instinct for things, stop and watch what other people do, be sensitive to offending others."

"You are kidding me. That's what you're worried about?"

"I'm worried about a lot of things."

"I've lost my entire world, everyone I knew, and you're concerned I'll *offend* someone?"

"I've hurt your feelings, and I didn't mean to do that."

"That's something, I suppose."

"But you'll thank me tomorrow or the next day or a week from now."

"I'm not so sure about that, Caleb, but there is one thing I do know." She stepped closer and looked down at her hair, which was still pulled forward and reached well past her waist. When she glanced back up at him, she saw that he was staring at it. She waited for him to raise his eyes to hers.

He swallowed and shifted from one foot to the other. "There was one thing you wanted to say?"

"*Ya.* Your old girlfriend?"

"Emily?"

"The one who told you that you were stubborn and old-fashioned."

"That would be Emily." He reached up and rubbed at the back of his neck. When he did, she smelled the soap he'd used earlier, noticed the muscles in his arm flex. His blond hair flopped forward, and it occurred to her that he was a nice-looking guy—nice-looking but with a terrible attitude and zero people skills.

"Between you and me—she was right. You are stubborn. You are old-fashioned, and you should keep your helpful hints to yourself."

And with that, she turned and fled down the hall, feeling better than she had since Caleb had rescued her from the snow.

The next morning, Caleb took as long with his chores as he dared. There was really no point in avoiding Rachel. She lived in their house now, and he would have to get used to her being around.

His mind darted back to her long hair. It wasn't brown exactly, or chestnut—more the warm color of honey. It had reminded him of kitten fur. As she'd stood next to him in the kitchen, he'd had the irrational urge to reach out and comb his fingers through it. The moonlight had softened her expression, and for a moment the look of vulnerability had vanished. Sure, it had vanished and been replaced with anger.

He remembered her parting words and almost laughed. He'd only been trying to help, but he'd never been particularly tactful. The fact that she'd called him on it…well, it showed that she had spunk and hopefully that she was healing. He decided to take it for a good sign rather than be offended.

When he walked into the kitchen, he noticed that her hair was properly braided, and she'd apparently borrowed one of his mother's *kapps*. Unfortunately, she wore the same dress as the day before. She gave him a pointed look, as if daring him to say something about it, but what could he say? It really wasn't his business. He'd done his duty by warning her. The rest was out of his hands.

Everyone sat at the table, waiting on him, so he washed his hands quickly and joined them. After a silent prayer, he began to fill his plate. He heaped on portions of scrambled eggs, sizzling sausage, homemade biscuits and breakfast potatoes, which were chopped and fried with onions and bell pepper.

"Someone's hungry this morning," Ida said.

"*Ya.* Mucking out stalls can do that to a man." He noticed that Rachel was eating, and she looked rested. "How are you feeling this morning, Rachel?"

"Better. Thank you, Caleb." Her tone was rather formal, and the look she gave him could freeze birds to a tree branch.

He nodded and focused on his plate of food. When he was nearly finished, he began to discuss the day's work with his father. They had a small enough farm— only seventy acres—but there was always work to do.

"Guess I'll finish mending that fence this morning."

"*Ya, gut* idea."

His mother jumped up and fetched the coffeepot from the stove burner. She refilled everyone's mugs, starting with Rachel's. Usually his mother threw in her opinion on their work, but she'd been deep in conversation with Rachel the entire meal. They'd been thick as thieves talking about who knew what—girl stuff, he supposed.

"Have you thought any more about the alpacas?" Caleb asked.

His father added creamer to his coffee. "I'm a little hesitant, to tell you the truth. I know nothing about the animals."

"They're a good investment," Caleb insisted. "Mr. Vann has decided he's too old to manage such a big farm."

Ida looked up in surprise. "It's hardly bigger than ours, and Mr. Vann is only—"

"Nearly seventy."

"Not so old, then." His father shared a smile with his mom. Must have been an old-people's joke, though his parents were only forty-eight.

"He has no children close enough to help on a daily basis," Caleb explained. "He's gifting the farm to his children and grandchildren, who will only use it for a weekend place. Obviously they can't keep the alpacas."

"I'm wondering if it's the best time of year to get into a new business."

"Better than planting season or harvesting, and he's letting them go cheap. I'm telling you, if we don't get them today, they'll probably be gone."

"Even a bargain costs money," John said.

"*Ya*, I'm aware of that, but we have plenty put back."

"What good are they, Caleb?" His mother held up a hand. "I'm not arguing with you. It's only that I know nothing about them."

"The yarn is quite popular," Rachel said.

Everyone turned to stare at her. She blushed the color of a pretty rose and added, "I don't know how I knew that."

"Did you maybe have alpacas before? At your parents' farm?"

"I don't—I don't think so, but I can remember the yarn. Spinners and knitters and even weavers use it."

"Any chance you recall how much trouble they are to raise?" His father laughed at his own joke, and then he reached across the table and patted her hand. "I don't expect you to answer that. I was only teasing because my son seems set on bringing strange animals onto our farm."

"I thought you were a traditionalist," Rachel said, then immediately pressed her fingers to her lips as if she wanted to pull back the words.

But if Caleb was worried he might have to answer that, might have to explain in front of his parents their conversation the night before, he was pleasantly mistaken.

Ida was up and clearing dishes, and she answered for him. "Oh, *ya*. In nearly every way that's true. Caleb is quite traditional."

"Unless it comes to animals," his father said. "We've tried camels."

"How was I to know they'd be so hard to milk?"

"And goats."

"We learned a lot that time."

"*Ya*, we learned if water can go through a fence, then so can a goat."

"We're a little off topic here." Caleb tried to ignore the fact that Rachel was now grinning at him as if she'd discovered the most amusing thing that she might insult him with later. "Let's just go look at the alpacas together. We could go this morning, and I'll fix the fence this afternoon."

"How about we do it the other way around?"

"Deal."

He was up and out of his chair, already glancing at the clock. If he worked quickly, they could be there before noon—surely before anyone else came along and bought the alpacas out from under their noses.

"Caleb, would you mind making sure that the front porch and steps are free of ice?"

"The front porch?"

"We're going to have visitors, and I don't want anyone slipping."

Visitors? On a Tuesday morning? "I was headed out to work on the fence line."

"And then look at alpacas. I heard."

He tugged on his ear. His mother was acting so strangely. Since when did she have weekday visitors? When had she ever asked him to clean off the front-porch steps?

"Shouldn't take but a few minutes," his father said. "Your mother wouldn't ask if she didn't need it."

The rebuke was mild, but still he felt his cheeks flushing.

"*Ya*, of course. Anything else?"

"You could move your muddy boots off the front porch, as well as that sanding project you've never finished."

"Did I miss something? Are we having Sunday service here on a Tuesday?" He meant it as a joke, but it came out as a whine.

Rachel jumped up to help his mother, not even attempting to hide her smile.

"Some ladies are stopping by." His mother reached up and patted his shoulder. "I just don't want them tripping over your things."

He rolled his eyes but assured her that he'd take care of it right away.

When he stepped out onto the front porch, his dad clapped him on the back. "Give them a little space. Your *mamm*, she's happy to have another girl around the place."

"*Ya*, that makes sense, but—"

"She's convinced that *Gotte* brought Rachel into our lives for a reason."

"To give me more work?"

"And, of course, we all want to make the transition easier for Rachel. This is bound to be a difficult time."

From the grin on Rachel's face, he didn't think it was as difficult as his father imagined, but instead of arguing with him, he found the stiff outdoor broom and began sweeping the steps to make sure there was no ice or water or snow there. *Woman's work*, he thought, but that wasn't what was bothering him. Change was in the air, and Caleb had never been one to embrace change— unless it was regarding farm animals.

In every other way, stubborn and old-fashioned was more his style.

Ida had shared with Rachel that a few ladies would be stopping by. "They heard about your situation and want to help."

She wasn't sure what that meant, but she'd nodded politely, and then Caleb had brought up alpacas, and the conversation had twisted and turned from there.

Now it was nearly noon, and she plopped onto the couch and stared at the items stacked on the coffee table.

Ida sat across from her, holding a steaming mug of

coffee. "Seems everyone from our community pitched in. It's *gut, ya*?"

"Of course. I'm a bit stunned. How did they even know that I'd need these things? How did they know I was here?"

"Word travels fast in an Amish community. Certainly you remember that."

"We used to call it the Amish grapevine."

Ida laughed. "I've heard that before, too, but 'grapevine' has a gossipy sound to it. This is really just neighbors helping neighbors."

Rachel picked the top dress off the pile of clothes. The color was midnight blue—Caleb would be happy about that—and the fabric was a good cotton that would last. It was also soft to the touch. She ran her hand across it, humbled by all that these women, who were strangers to her, had given.

"We'll need to take those in, of course. You're shorter and smaller than Rebekah's girls."

"Won't they need these?"

"Not likely, both have put on a good bit of weight since marrying, and that was before they were expecting her first grandchildren. No, I don't think they'll be needing them back."

There were underclothes, *kapps*, two outdoor bonnets and a coat. All except the underclothes were used, but in good condition. Someone had brought a Bible and a journal for writing in. She thought those might come in handy. Dr. Gold had mentioned that writing a little every day might help her memories return. There was also a new scarf and gloves, knitted in a dark gray that had a touch of shimmer to it. "This is beautiful work."

"Melinda can do wonders with a knitting needle. I've always been more of a crochet person myself."

Rachel stood up, went to the room she was staying in and returned with the blue scarf she'd apparently been wearing when Caleb had found her. No coat, but a scarf—strange indeed. "I think—I think I might be a knitter."

"That's why you knew about the alpaca yarn."

"Maybe. I think so. I know this is called a stockinette pattern—you alternate rows of knitting with rows of purling." She closed her eyes, could almost see herself adjusting the tension in her yarn, squinting at a pattern, knitting needles flying. She could be imagining, or she could be remembering. There was no way to know.

"Are you remembering anything else?"

"Only that this—" She ran her fingers over the scarf, then draped it around her neck. "It seems very familiar."

"That's a beginning."

"If only I could remember more, but when I try, the headaches return."

Ida walked over to the bookcase and brought back the packet of information from the doctor at the hospital. Rachel had already rifled through it twice. There were instructions, what to expect, warning signs, as well as two cards—one for her next appointment with Dr. Gold and another card with the name and contact information for a Dr. Michie. She'd spoken with the doctor a few minutes before leaving the hospital. She was a counselor of some sort and had told Rachel to call her if she'd like to make an appointment.

Ida sat beside Rachel on the couch and they both stared down at the top page.

Ida read aloud from the sheet. "'Symptoms of a concussion include brief loss of consciousness.'"

"Check."

"'Memory problems.'"

"We all know I have that."

"'Confusion.'"

Rachel leaned forward, propped her elbows on her knees and pressed her fingertips to her forehead. "Sometimes, when I can't remember how I know something, I feel terribly confused."

Ida nodded and continued with the list. "'Drowsiness or feeling sluggish.'"

"Twice this morning I went back and laid down on the bed for a few minutes."

"Only because I insisted. You need to recognize when things are overwhelming you. It's important for a woman to learn to take care of herself. You're no use to your family—"

"I don't have one."

"Or anyone else if you allow yourself to become ill or exhausted."

Rachel heard the concern in Ida's voice, but she couldn't bring herself to meet her gaze. "I'm batting a thousand, as my *bruder* would say..."

She slapped her hand over her mouth.

Ida reached over and clutched her hand. "That's *gut*, Rachel. You're starting to remember. That's a *gut* sign."

"I suppose."

"Can you remember his name?"

"Nein."

"Older or younger?"

She closed her eyes and tried to picture her family, tried to recall anything from her past, but to no avail.

Her heart was racing and her mind was spinning off in a dozen directions, but she couldn't quite grasp even one solid piece of information about her former life—other than she had a brother. Was he worried? Was he looking for her?

Finally, she motioned for Ida to continue with the list of symptoms. They knew she had a concussion, the doctor had confirmed as much, but it helped to know that the things she was feeling and experiencing weren't unusual.

"'Dizziness or blurred vision.'"

"A little yesterday, when I first woke up in the hospital."

"'Headache.'"

"*Ya*, especially when I try to remember."

"'Nausea or vomiting.'"

"Not since I started eating."

"'Sensitivity to light.'"

"That's on there?" She scooted closer and peered at the sheet. "I tried going outside for a few moments earlier, but the sunshine felt like a pitchfork in my brain. I found myself wishing I had my sunglasses."

"Another puzzle piece. You have a *bruder* and you wore sunglasses."

"Doesn't everyone?"

"Perhaps." Ida tapped the last item on the list. "What about balance problems? Any trouble there?"

"I'm not sure. Let's check." Rachel jumped up and pretended to walk a straight line, holding her hands out to the side. She pivoted and started back toward Ida, touching her nose with first her right and then left index finger as she walked. Ida began to laugh, and then Rachel began to laugh, and soon they were giggling like schoolgirls.

And, of course, that was the moment that Caleb walked inside, a frown pulling down the corners of his mouth. Why did he always seem to be disapproving of her? She pitied the woman that did decide to marry him or even date him. Caleb Wittmer might be a good man, but he wasn't much fun to be around, and life should include some fun. Shouldn't it?

"We're about to head over to see the alpacas."

"Oh, well, I hope it goes well, dear."

"Actually I was wondering…"

"About?"

"Lunch."

Ida started laughing again, and then she spread her arms to encompass the pile of goods their neighbors had brought. "We've been pretty busy in here."

"I see that."

"Our neighbors brought all of these things for Rachel."

"Wunderbaar."

"Honestly I forgot about making lunch, but I'll throw some sandwiches together."

Caleb nodded as if that made sense. His mother brushed past him, humming as she went into the kitchen.

"Let me guess." Rachel couldn't have stopped the smile spreading across her face if she'd tried, which she didn't. "You're not used to eating sandwiches."

"Actually I can't remember the last time *Mamm* didn't have lunch waiting on the table."

Rachel attempted to make sympathetic noises, but it probably came out like she'd managed to choke on something. She knew she should keep her mouth shut. Instead she said, "Men can make a sandwich, too, Caleb. Maybe you should give your *mamm* a little bit of a break here. Having me around? It's a lot of extra work."

He narrowed his eyes and pulled in a deep breath.

Rachel immediately regretted baiting him.

"Your community has been very nice. They even brought me some appropriate clothing." Oops. She'd done it again.

Instead of aggravating Caleb, he seemed to relax. Perhaps poking at one another felt like safe ground to him. "That is a *gut* thing. I see you even have several *kapps* and bonnets there."

He picked one up. Unfortunately, it happened to be on top of the pile of underclothes. When he glanced down and saw the stack of underthings, he dropped the bonnet, turned a bright shade of red and then pivoted and fled from the room.

Rachel grabbed a pillow and buried her face in it so that he couldn't hear her laughter. Which felt so much better than worrying about what Caleb thought of her— that question was behind the laughter. She didn't want to think about that, though, or about why it mattered.

She needed to remember who she was. Borrowed clothes, a guest room in someone else's house and Caleb looking over her shoulder to see if she was following the rules were not how she wanted to live the rest of her life.

Chapter Three

Caleb bought the seven alpacas that afternoon.

His father had finally said, "You saved the money yourself. If it's what you want, then give it a try."

"Strangest animal I've ever seen" was his mother's only comment.

Caleb spent the rest of the week making sure the alpacas had adequate space in the barn, reinforcing fencing where he would pasture them and generally getting to know the strange beasts.

His parents came out once a day to check on the animals and his best friend, Gabriel, had been by twice. Mostly he'd laughed at Caleb's feeble attempts to interact with them.

As for Rachel, she hadn't stepped outside of the house at all. If anything, she'd seemed physically worse on Wednesday and Thursday. At one point, his *mamm* had walked down to the phone shack and contacted the doctor, who had called in a prescription for nausea and told her to be patient. "These things take time" were the doctor's exact words.

So Caleb was surprised when he was in the field

with the alpacas on Friday morning and looked up to see Rachel leaning against the fence. She wore a proper dress and coat, plus one of the outer bonnets she'd been given, though there was little wind and the sun had melted away every last trace of snow. She also sported sunglasses, an old pair of his mother's if he remembered correctly. In the crook of her arm she was carrying a bowl that his mother used to dump scraps into.

"Nice to see you outside."

"If I sit in the house one more day, I might go crazy. One can only read so much or do so many crossword puzzles."

"I wouldn't know."

"What's that supposed to mean?"

"Only that I work every day from sunrise until dark."

"Life of a farmer, I guess."

"Amish women work hard, too. At least most of them do."

"Kind of hard to find a job if you can't remember anything more than your first name."

Caleb shrugged. Rachel could find work if she wanted it. They both knew it. Instead of defending herself further, she changed the subject.

"Have you named them?"

"*Nein.* We don't name our cows."

"I don't see any cows."

"We only have three—all dairy cows. They're in the east pasture."

"Oh. I guess I haven't been in that direction yet." She reached out her hand and one of the alpacas moseyed over to sniff at her palm.

"I'd call you Mocha."

The alpaca stood completely still and allowed her to rub its top notch of hair.

"How'd you do that? They won't let me within five feet of them."

When the male alpaca began to crunch on something, one of the females bounded over to join him. Soon he could barely see Rachel because the entire herd of alpacas had congregated near the fence. Caleb walked over to see what she was giving him.

"Apple slices?"

"*Ya*. Your *mamm* is making an apple pie, but she didn't want to include the skins. It seems like I always did when I baked a pie…" She shook her head back and forth, as if she could rattle the memory free.

Caleb scratched at his jaw. "I didn't think of giving them scraps."

"Makes sense, though. Most animals enjoy apple slices. We had a dog once that loved them."

Her head jerked up and she met Caleb's gaze, surprise coloring her features.

"You're remembering more every day."

"Small inconsequential things. It's frustrating."

"Not to my alpacas."

She smiled at that, and Caleb felt inexplicably better. He didn't pretend to understand Rachel, but he somehow thought of himself as responsible for her. Perhaps that was normal considering he'd found her in the snow only a few days before.

"Did you get a good deal on the animals?"

"I think so. Less than three thousand dollars for all seven, and there are two females."

"Hopefully you'll have baby alpacas running around by spring."

"That's the plan."

"Do you expect they'll be much work?"

"Not according to Mr. Vann. They mainly eat hay and grass, though some mineral supplements are good, too."

"So you won't be spending much money to maintain them."

"Nein. Also, they don't bite or butt or spit. I tried raising a llama once, but that didn't go so well."

Rachel crossed her arms on the fence and rested her head on top of them, watching the group of alpacas dart away and then flop and roll in a patch of dirt. He'd seen them do that before, but watching Rachel watching them, seeing the smile grow on her face, he realized for the first time what funny animals they were.

"They're herd animals, so it's a good thing I was able to buy seven."

"I think you made a good business decision, Caleb. You'll know for sure once you shear them, but my guess is that you'll make a nice return on your investment."

"Mr. Vann said to watch the top notch. If the hair grows to cover their eyes, I'm supposed to have it cut, which will mean learning to do it myself because I'm not about to pay someone else to do it."

Rachel covered her mouth to hide a giggle, which Caleb heard nonetheless.

"What's so funny?"

"Explain that to me," she said.

"Explain what?"

"You're so old-fashioned about other things." She held up a hand when he began to protest. "You admitted it yourself, the first night I was here. The night that you told me about your last girlfriend."

"She wasn't right about everything."

"But you said…what was it? 'My normal personality is bullheaded and old-fashioned.'"

"*Ya.* I suppose it's true."

"Not exactly unusual among the Amish."

"Oh, you remember that, do you?"

"So why are you such a risk taker as far as animals?"

"Crops, too," he admitted. He'd been watching the animals, but now he turned to study Rachel. "I'll answer your question, but first tell me why you want to know."

"Curious, I guess. Sort of like your alpacas."

The horses were grazing in the adjacent pasture. The gelding had wandered close to the fence separating it from the alpacas. The horse was focused on the winter grass, but one of the tan alpacas had zeroed in on the horse. It stuck its nose through the fence, then jumped back, jumped almost vertically. Which caused the other alpacas to trot over, and then they were all gawking at the horse and making a high-pitched noise that sounded like a cat with its tail caught in a door.

"So you're not asking merely to give me grief?"

"Not at all." With her fingers, she crossed her heart. "Promise."

He leaned against the fence, studying the animals but thinking of the woman standing beside him. Rachel was a jumbled mix of paradoxes. One moment she seemed vulnerable, the next fiercely independent, and then sometimes she was quietly curious.

Glancing at her, he realized—not for the first time—what a beautiful woman she was. Probably back in her own community she had a boyfriend who was wondering what had happened to her. The thought made him uncomfortable, as if they should be doing more to return her to her home. But what could they do?

Nothing, so far as he knew, so instead he settled for being honest and answering her question.

"I like the Plain life. I've seen my fair share of folks leave our faith—about half of them came back, tails tucked between their legs. The other half? They either never visit their family at all—"

"Is it allowed?"

"Oh, *ya*. Our bishop encourages families to support one another, even when a member chooses a different path."

Rachel nodded, as if that made sense.

"These people I'm thinking of, they have a standing invitation to come home and see their loved ones."

"But they don't?"

"Most don't. The ones that do, they seem put out that they have to leave their cell phone in the car."

"Are you speaking from personal experience?"

"You're asking if anyone in my family has gone over to the *Englisch* side?" Caleb ran his hand along the top rail of the metal fence—it was smooth and cold to the touch. "Two cousins, on my mother's side."

"So that makes you conservative…as far as people are concerned."

"I think being Plain means we stand for something. We stand for a different lifestyle. Once we start making compromises, there's no difference between us and the *Englisch*—in that case, who wouldn't leave?"

Rachel was shaking her head, her bonnet strings swaying back and forth, but she smiled and said, "All right. I've never heard it expressed that way before, but—"

"You might have. Maybe you don't remember."

"Good point. So you're conservative because you think it's good for families and believers."

"Right."

"But the farming? And animals?"

"In business you want to be conservative—for sure and certain you do."

"But?"

"It's exciting to try something new. *Ya?* Look at those animals. They seem like giant poodles to me. Who figured out that their wool would be a good crop?"

"Caleb, you surprise me."

"Ya?" He reached forward and brushed some grass off her coat sleeve, no doubt left by one of his alpacas that had been nosing closer for apple peels. "Is that *gut* or bad?"

"Both. The alpacas will be entertaining."

They'd returned to flopping down in the dirt.

"Your herd looks like they will produce a variety of coffee colors."

"Coffee, huh?"

"Something *Englischers* love—lots of browns and tans and mochas and cappuccinos. Maybe even a cinnamon hue on that far one."

"Cappuccino?" He could feel the frown forming on his lips. No doubt she loved visiting a coffee shop and wasting her money.

"Plus their fiber is hypoallergenic, which is what makes it very popular."

"Funny that you know that."

She simply shrugged.

"I know nothing about shearing, but I can learn."

"Do you have a local library?"

"Sure."

"You can search how to do that on their computers."

He felt something freeze inside of him. This happened

every time he began to feel comfortable with Rachel. She said or did something that reminded him she didn't belong here and probably wouldn't be staying. He stepped away from the fence, so now they were facing each other, though Rachel was a good head shorter than he was.

"We don't use the computers."

"Why?" She cocked her head and looked genuinely puzzled.

"Because we choose not to. We're *Plain*..." He couldn't help emphasizing the last word, though he realized it sounded patronizing.

"Uh-huh. Well, I can tell you're getting aggravated, so I suppose I should go back inside."

"We just talked about what it means to be Plain, and then you throw out a comment about using computers."

"There's nothing wrong with a computer, Caleb." She stepped closer, right up into his personal space, and stared up at him.

He took a step back.

"Computers aren't evil."

"Never said they were, but they're not Plain."

"A computer isn't going to cause anyone to leave the faith."

"It could. The things you can see on one...well, it's like bait to our *youngies*..."

"Of which you are one."

He laughed at that. "Turned twenty-five last year."

"Me, too."

They both froze, the argument suddenly forgotten.

"Another piece of the puzzle of Rachel," he said softly.

She glanced at him uncertainly, a range of emotions playing across her face, and then she turned and wandered back into the house, pausing now and again to look back at the alpacas.

Rachel spent the rest of Friday morning helping Ida, but honestly there wasn't much to do for a family of three—four if she counted herself. Was she a part of Ida's family? Was this her home now? When would she remember her past?

And beneath those questions were Caleb's words, mocking her.

Amish women work hard, too. At least most of them do.

Did he think she liked not being able to remember her own last name or where she was from? Did he think she enjoyed being ill?

"The headaches are better, *ya*?" Ida was crocheting a gray-and-black winter scarf for Caleb. She only brought it out during the day, not wanting him to see it until Christmas morning.

Rachel was sitting and staring at the crochet needle that Ida had given her. She'd even shown her how to use it, but the rhythm and stitch pattern seemed completely foreign. If she'd crocheted in her other life, she certainly couldn't remember doing so.

"Some."

"That's *gut*. You're a little better every day. You could be entirely well by Christmas."

"Does your community celebrate on December twenty-fifth or on January sixth?"

"Both. The older generation—older than me even, they prefer Old Christmas."

"Probably includes Caleb."

"Caleb likes both holidays—mainly because I cook his favorite dishes."

"I wish I could remember how to use this." Rachel stared at the crochet needle. "I wish I remembered something useful."

"That seems to happen when you're not thinking about it." She pointed to the journal that contained the list that Rachel had made. The list was pitifully short, in her opinion. She opened the journal and stared down at the first page.

My name is Rachel.
I have a brother.
I know about alpaca wool.
Used to wear sunglasses?
I'm 25 years old.

"Those things could describe a lot of women."

"And yet they describe you, and *Gotte* made you special and unique."

"Now you're trying to cheer me up."

"Indeed." Ida peered at her over the reading glasses she wore while crocheting. The frames were a pretty blue, which probably irked Caleb to no end. A blue dress was out of the question—blue frames couldn't be far behind.

"Do you know what I think is wrong with you?"

Rachel nearly choked on the water she'd been sipping. She'd known Ida for only less than a week, and yet already she knew the woman had a gentle spirit—one that wasn't critical.

"What's wrong with me?"

Now Ida was smiling. "Uh-huh."

"Tell me, Ida. Because it may just be that my brain is bruised, but I feel all out of sorts."

"You have cabin fever."

"Pardon me?"

"Cabin fever. I used to suffer from it something terrible when Caleb was a babe. That was a hard winter, and we were inside—in this very house—too much. Finally, his father came into the kitchen one morning and told me that he had finished all of his work in the barn."

"A farmer's work is never done…"

"Exactly. When John came in that morning, he claimed he'd finished the work that *had* to be done, took the babe from my arms and told me to go to town."

"And did it help?"

"Immensely. After that, one day a week he'd come in and take care of Caleb for a few hours while I went on little errands."

"So I need to go on little errands?"

"Wouldn't hurt." Ida dropped her crochet work in her lap and pulled a scrap of paper from her apron pocket. "Here's some things I need from the general store. It's on the main road. You won't have any trouble finding it. While you're out, maybe you can find something whimsical to do."

"Whimsical?"

"Impulsive. Something you hadn't planned on. Life on a farm can be awfully predictable. A surprise, even a little one, can brighten the spirit."

"How am I supposed to get there?"

"John told me he'd bring around the buggy after lunch."

"What if I don't remember how to drive a buggy?"

"We won't know that until you try. If you don't remember, then I'll ask Caleb to go with you."

The rest of the morning sped by and suddenly lunch

was over and the buggy and horse were waiting near the front porch.

Maybe it was the thought of a little freedom, or perhaps it was fear that Caleb would be saddled with her for an afternoon when he'd rather be with his alpacas—he'd frowned fiercely when Ida shared their plan during lunch—but whatever the cause, Rachel was determined to drive the buggy herself. She needn't have worried. As soon as she climbed up into the buggy, something deep inside of her brain took over.

Her hands picked up the reins.

She clucked to the horse.

Her spirit soared, and she pulled away.

Ida had given her an envelope with cash in it and drawn a crude map on the back of the list. The way to the general store was simple and consisted of driving down the lane to the main road, making a right and heading into town. Rachel suspected the map was in case she forgot how to get home, but her confidence had surged as soon as she'd begun driving the buggy. She didn't think she'd be getting lost.

The dark cloud that had been hovering over her mood lifted by the time she hit the main road. Farms dotted the way into town, and many had Christmas displays in the yards. *Englisch* homes had lights strung across shrubs and trees. She wondered what they'd look like at night.

Other houses sported giant inflatable yard decorations. There were large white polar bears wearing red neckties, yellow cartoon characters with blue pants and round eyeglasses that she had seen on *Englisch* coloring books, and even reindeer pulling a sleigh. A few Amish homes had wooden nativities, and their porches were decorated with green cedar wrapped around the porch railing.

As she neared town, she passed a sign that read Welcome to Montgomery, Indiana. The name didn't ring any bells. But then, she already knew she wasn't from here.

So how had she happened on the road that led to Caleb's home?

Where was she from?

In town, the main road was filled with other buggies as well as cars. She saw even more decorations, including festive window displays, city banners wishing everyone "Happy Holidays" and churches reminding people when their Christmas services would be held. It was only December seventh, but it seemed that everyone was getting ready for the holiday early.

She was waiting at a signal light when a car of *Englischers* pulled up beside her, and a young child waved. She waved back as they pulled away. If it hadn't been for the child, she wouldn't have been looking in that direction, but she was...and so she saw the sign that said Montgomery Public Library.

She was in the wrong lane. She had to drive another block before turning, but the entire time she could hear Caleb's words in her ears.

Amish women work hard, too. At least most of them do.

He might not want to use the *Englisch* computers to learn about his new alpaca herd, but she was more than willing to look for a job on them. Something told her that if she wanted to move forward, the internet would be the place to start.

Find a job. Earn some money. Remember who she was.

It was a short list, and suddenly Rachel was sure it was one she could conquer.

Chapter Four

Rachel's library search was not fruitful.

First of all, the library was small—smaller than she had imagined. The room was about the size of Ida's sitting room. The walls were lined with bookcases that were filled to capacity with books, but there wasn't exactly a large variety of material and much of it looked quite dated. Worse, there were only two computers. Both were being used when she walked in, so she had to wait. While she did, she perused the bookshelves. There was a single shelf with books labeled Christian Fiction. She thought to check one out, then realized she didn't have any identification.

The librarian had been watching her—she was an older lady with shoulder-length silver hair and was wearing a bright red sweater that said Ho Ho Ho across the front. She stood about only five feet tall, and Rachel couldn't help envisioning one of the elves she'd seen as part of a lawn display on her drive into town.

"Problem, dear?"

"Only that I don't…well, I don't have any identification. I'm staying with John and Ida Wittmer."

"You must be the girl Caleb found in the snow."

"*Ya.* Unless he found two, and I haven't met the other one yet."

"I'm pretty sure it was you—Amish, young, pretty and with freckles." She walked over to Rachel, patted her on the arm and smiled. "I mean no offense, dear. You're quite the topic of conversation around our little township—a real Christmas mystery."

"I never thought of it that way." Rachel turned back to the books, allowed her fingertips to caress the spines. Had she always liked to read? What were her favorite types of books?

"You can pick out up to three items."

"But I don't have an identification card."

"So you mentioned."

"I don't even remember my own last name, and… and I don't have a home address."

"For now, your home address is Ida and John's place, which I know because they both have a card here."

"They do? I thought Caleb said…"

"I'm well aware of Caleb's opinion on the matter, but I suspect one day he will marry and perhaps his wife will be able to soften that stubborn spirit."

Rachel didn't know how to answer that. From what she'd seen of Caleb Wittmer it would take more than a wife to change his attitudes—it would take divine intervention.

"As far as your last name, we'll just put Rachel for now. I make up the entire library staff—well, me and one part-time girl who works a few hours in the afternoon. So there's no one to tell me what I can and can't do. I'm Mary Agnes Putnam, by the way, but most people just call me Mary Agnes."

The woman was as good as her word. While Rachel picked out one novel and a slim volume of poems by William Blake, Mary Agnes printed her a library card on an old printer, which sounded as if it was in distress. Rachel looked over a few cooking books, several historical tomes and some children's titles. As she was walking toward the checkout desk, she spied a pile of books with the word *Self-help* neatly printed and taped to the wall beside it. She dug through the stack and came up with *Crocheting for Dummies*. Maybe she'd feel useful if she could at least use Ida's crochet needle properly.

Mary Agnes checked out her material, and Rachel confessed, "I came in to use the computer."

"Indeed? We get that a lot around here."

"Maybe I should come back." She glanced over at the two old gentlemen who were still at their monitors.

"I'll take care of those two for you. They're playing chess—with one another—on the computer!" She leaned forward and lowered her voice. "We have a chessboard on the game shelf, and even a table where they can play, but both Albert and Wayne say they need to learn to travel the *information highway*. That's what they call it. So they play chess every day on the monitors. Fancy the things that people do."

Mary Agnes ran off the two men, who claimed it was time for their lunch, anyway. She showed Rachel how to log on and directed her to Montgomery's virtual job-search board.

But thirty minutes on the computer only increased Rachel's frustration. She couldn't fill in any applications with no last name. She didn't know what her educational level was. Ida had mentioned that most Amish students attended school through eighth grade. Had she?

Who knew? Maybe she'd lived in a district that went to school through twelfth grade like the *Englischers*. Did any Amish do that? She certainly couldn't recall her employment history, though if she was twenty-five she must have worked somewhere.

Sighing in frustration, she logged off, picked up her three books and thanked Mary Agnes for her help. She stepped out into a day that felt more like fall than winter. She should go on to the store and pick up the items on Ida's list, but then she remembered Ida telling her to take her time. What was it she had said?

Do something whimsical.

She couldn't imagine what that might be, so she walked over to the parking area and checked on the buggy horse, who was contentedly cropping grass.

Whimsical?

There was a park bench in the middle of the grassy area on the north side of the library. No one else was around, so she made her way across the small area and sat down, eventually putting her head back and closing her eyes. The sun felt good on her face, and some of the tension in her shoulders eased—as long as she didn't think about her predicament.

Instead of worrying, she focused on the word *predicament*. She could practically see the definition printed on a page. *An unpleasantly difficult, perplexing or dangerous situation.* Now, why could she remember that and not her own name? She was puzzling over that enormous question when someone cleared his throat.

She opened her eyes to find Bishop Amos standing beside her.

"Oh. I didn't hear you walk up." She jumped up, but

Amos waved her back onto the bench and sat down beside her.

"This is one of my favorite places in Montgomery."

"It is?"

"I can see and hear what's going on, but I'm away from the sidewalk or street. Sometimes I bring birdseed and scatter it out in front of me."

"The sunshine feels *gut*."

"*Ya?* And how do you feel?"

Rachel could have lied and said she was fine, but something about the way Amos asked the question and waited for an answer told her he was really interested. So she found herself confessing to her frustration at not being able to remember things, her guilt that Ida and John had done so much for her, and her conversation with Caleb over how she needed to get a job.

"He said that, did he? That you should go to work… today?"

"Not in so many words, but it's what he meant."

Amos was maybe the oldest bishop that Rachel had ever known. His skin looked like fine tissue paper, and the only hair on his head were wispy strands at the very top. He had giant white bushy eyebrows that wiggled up and down when he smiled, which he did a lot. Rachel had met him only twice, and already she knew that he was *that* kind of bishop—the kind, fatherly, compassionate type.

"Caleb's a good boy," he finally said, folding both hands on top of his walking cane and leaning forward to stare down at the ground.

Rachel glanced down to see what he was looking at and spied a trail of ants marching beneath their feet. Funny how she hadn't noticed them before.

"Can't be easy, I imagine." Amos paused, as if he was waiting for her to agree.

"What can't be easy?"

"Being an only child in an Amish family. It's unusual. You're the odd man out. Might make a person keep to himself. Might make him more stubborn." Amos glanced sideways at her and the bushy eyebrows arched up and down again.

"Yes, I can understand that. What I don't understand is why does he have to take it out on me? Why be so insulting? I'm not a lazy person."

"Of course you're not."

"And I'd get a job if I could."

"Having something to do does add value to our days."

"But no one will hire me. I was just inside looking on the computers, and I can't get past the first page of the application. It keeps reminding me to fill in all the boxes, when I don't know what to put in them. You know things like 'last name' and 'address' and 'place of birth.'"

"A computer can be good for some things," Amos admitted. "I myself like to check the weather on it."

He straightened up, popping his back in the process, and smiled at Rachel as if he'd answered all of her questions when, in fact, he hadn't.

"You use the computers?"

"*Ya.* We're not so backward here in Montgomery. Personally, I hope the day never comes when I see one in an Amish home, but many things are useful in small doses—automobiles, telephones, computers. They're useful for certain things and certain times."

"What do you mean, exactly?"

"Only that in some instances it's best to do a thing face-to-face."

"You think I should go knocking on business doors and ask them to hire me? Why would they when I'm a complete stranger to them and have no references?"

"I'll be your reference."

"Thank you, Amos, but I don't think—"

"There's a quilt shop here in town, owned by a nice Mennonite woman."

"I can't remember if I know how to quilt."

"And there's Gasthof Amish Village."

"What is that? I saw a sign for it as I came into town."

Instead of answering, he said, "I know the owner there as well as the person who manages the auction house."

"We have an auction house?"

"Yes, I think one of those might be a good answer for your dilemma, Rachel."

"You mean for Caleb's dilemma."

"Oh, you can't do this because Caleb wants you to—or because you think it will please Ida or John or even me."

"I suppose I could use the money."

"More than that, you need to listen to your heart." Amos tapped his chest. "Your heart is asking something of you, Rachel. Your job is to listen and pray—then and only then should you decide what you will do."

"And in the meantime?"

"In the meantime, I'll check around. We'll talk on Sunday and see if what your heart is saying matches up with any opportunities I've found."

He tapped his walking stick against the ground, bounded off the bench with the energy of a man twenty years younger and settled his hat onto his head. "*Gotte* be with you, Rachel."

"And with you." The words slipped off her tongue, unbidden, remembered.

* * *

Caleb was in the back pasture, mending yet another section of fence that the alpacas had managed to push through.

"Worse than goats?" Gabriel asked.

"Maybe not worse, but as bad…" Caleb wiped the back of his arm across his brow. Sweating in December was probably a bad sign. His mother would say it meant a blue norther was waiting around the corner.

Gabriel moved next to him and held the fence post in place while he twisted the strands of wire. When they'd finished, they sat on top of a stack of small hay squares, watching the alpacas.

"Strange animals," Gabriel said.

"Indeed."

"Are they growing on you?"

"I haven't asked to get my money back yet, if that's what you're asking."

"Is that an option?"

"Probably not."

Gabriel pulled a piece of hay from the bale and stuck it in his mouth. They'd been friends as long as Caleb could remember. Gabriel was the brother Caleb had never had.

"Ida stopped by to see my *fraa*, told her that Rachel had taken a real liking to the animals. Even named them all."

"And what did Beth think about that?"

"That it was a *gut* sign. That maybe it meant she wouldn't run away."

Caleb snorted. "Why would she run? She's living a pretty sweet life here."

"Is that a problem?"

"*Nein.*"

"Only—"

"I suggested she get a job."

"Huh-oh."

"And she took offense."

"I wonder why."

"Come on, Gabriel. We are Plain and we work. It's what we do. It's not like we can sit around all day and watch television or play on our cell phones."

"Saw my cousin with one of those the other day. I've no idea how he affords it."

"My point is that my comment wasn't out of line. I was trying to be helpful."

"Ah."

"What does 'ah' mean?"

"It's what Amish men do, according to Beth. We give our opinion, even when no one has asked for it, and then say that we're trying to help."

"Only Amish men?"

Gabriel laughed, and the easiness of it, the way it went all the way to his eyes, stirred an unfamiliar sense of envy in Caleb. Between the two of them Caleb had always been the first to do things. He was the first to shave, the first to ask a girl on a date and the first to be dumped by a girl. He'd joined the church a year before Gabriel. He was two inches taller than his best friend and twenty pounds heavier—muscle, not extra pound-age. He was smarter in school, faster in sports and a better farmer.

None of that mattered.

They were best friends in every sense of the word.

Maybe he'd considered himself special in some way

because he was an only child. It could, after all, be both a blessing and a curse.

Gabriel was the middle child in a family of seven. He'd always worn well-patched hand-me-down clothes. He didn't purchase his own buggy until he'd married, and he'd never had his own bedroom. None of that seemed to bother Gabriel, though.

Things didn't matter to Gabriel. People did.

He'd met Beth and they'd courted and married and had a child. In one year, he'd achieved everything Caleb had dreamed of, everything that had slipped through his fingers when Emily had walked away after proclaiming him stubborn and strong-willed and impossible to be with. He hadn't shared that last part with Rachel. The memory of those words still stung, and perhaps that was why he had stopped courting. Finding someone to share his life with hadn't happened, and he was beginning to doubt it ever would.

"Beth has another theory." An alpaca had wandered closer to them. Gabriel reached out to touch it, but the animal jumped, screeched its cat sound and bounded away.

"Why am I worried?"

"It's about Rachel."

"Beth has only met her once. How can she have a theory?"

"I suppose it's actually about you."

"Worse still." Caleb crossed his arms, fighting off the urge to be offended. "Well, let's have it. Beth has proved her wisdom by marrying you. Perhaps I should listen to her."

"Compliments won't make this any better." Gabriel sat up, propped his elbows on his knees and interlaced

his fingers. "Her first theory is that you were used to being an only."

"An only?"

"Only child. And we both know your *mamm* has always wanted a daughter around the house."

"Remember the year she set me up on dates once a month? Talk about a nightmare."

"But now she has a girl in the house...one that *Gotte* practically brought to your doorstep."

"She wandered here. Remember? If I hadn't seen her when I did, she probably would have kept on walking."

"If you hadn't seen her, hadn't rescued her, she might have died there in the snow. Remember it reached into the twenties that night, and you said yourself she had no coat."

Caleb didn't pretend to understand the how or why of Rachel's appearance, so instead he motioned for Gabriel to continue.

"So now your *mamm* has a daughter, your *dat* has someone to dote on and suddenly you're not the center of their attention."

"A welcome relief, I can tell you."

"Uh-huh, and yet your mood hasn't exactly improved."

"So I'm what...jealous?"

Gabriel shrugged. "It's only a theory—Beth's theory, not mine."

"Ridiculous."

"If you say so."

"And her second theory?"

Gabriel stood and brushed hay from his pants. When he glanced up, there was a twinkle in his eye and a smile tugging at his lips. "Easy. That you're falling for Rachel."

"Falling for her?"

"Romantically speaking."

"Rachel?"

"Love does strange things to a man. Trust me, I know. Muddles your thoughts, changes your appetite, feels like the flu at times. It can certainly put you in a foul mood."

Instead of answering that, because it was too preposterous to merit a reply, Caleb stood as well and began gathering up his tools.

"Told you…it's Beth's theory, not mine."

Caleb grunted.

"Though it does make some sense. You said yourself she's beautiful."

How he wished he'd never shared that opinion with his best friend.

"No one would blame you."

Once Caleb had everything in the wooden toolbox with the handy carrying handle, he turned and walked toward the barn.

"Where are you going?" Gabriel called after him.

But Caleb only offered a backhanded wave.

As if it wasn't bad enough that his life had been disrupted by a mysterious Amish woman, now he had people gossiping that he was in love. Well, he had an answer for that. One way or another he would find where Rachel belonged and he'd take her there, and then his life would return to normal.

At least that was his plan.

It didn't actually improve his mood, but it gave him something else to focus on.

Chapter Five

If Rachel had hoped to spend Saturday inside with Ida, teaching herself to crochet and writing in her journal, she was sadly mistaken.

"A cold front is blowing through tonight. I need you to help Caleb with this list of to-dos while the weather is good."

This was presented to her as they were eating breakfast, and she'd made the mistake of glancing over at Caleb, who had rolled his eyes. So he wasn't any happier about the day's agenda than she was.

John didn't seem to notice the tension in the air. "I'd help if I could, but I promised Big Atlee that I'd help him mend his barn's south wall."

"I could do that," Caleb said.

"*Nein.* Help your mother. You know how she loves Christmas."

"Big Atlee?" Rachel asked.

"Oh, *ya*. We have a Big Atlee—he's bigger than Caleb even, and Little Atlee…"

"Who isn't really little," Ida pointed out.

"But smaller than Big Atlee, and then there's Limping Atlee."

"You actually call him Limping Atlee?"

"He doesn't mind. Thinks it's clever." John smiled at her and drained his coffee cup. "You know how it is with the Amish—no need for new fancy names when old ones will do, even if it means having two or three in the same family."

Rachel watched as Ida followed her husband into the mudroom. They spoke softy as he donned his jacket and hat, and then Ida stood on tiptoe to kiss him lightly on the lips. For a moment, his arms tightened around her waist, and a smile spread across her lips, and Ida looked like the young woman she must have once been.

"They're romantic fools," Caleb said, nodding toward his parents.

"I think it's sweet."

"*Ya*, until they forget and hold hands in public."

Rachel might have thought that Caleb was being harsh, but his ears had turned red. Was he actually embarrassed that his parents sometimes showed their affection for one another? "What's wrong with holding hands?"

"It's just not what we do."

"Is that so?"

"I love my parents, but they sometimes forget that others are watching. They also have a tendency to butt into other people's business."

She didn't know how to answer that, so she stood to begin clearing the dishes.

"Meet me in the barn when you're done," he said, and then Caleb, too, was gone.

Rachel took her time with the washing and drying.

By the time Ida came back in, she had the kitchen looking positively sparkly.

"Oh, dear, I didn't mean for you to do all the work. I just wanted to walk John out to his buggy."

"How long have you been married?"

"Twenty-eight years, and it's been a journey, let me tell you. We've had our ups and downs, good years and bad." Ida was looking out the window, watching John drive down the lane. When she turned back toward Rachel, her expression had become more serious. "Caleb gets his stubborn streak honestly, and it's not from me. They are both good men, though. And I've never once doubted that John loved me. What more could a woman ask for?"

To remember her own name?

To go home for Christmas?

To know where home was?

But all those things sounded whiny in her head, so Rachel didn't say them. Instead she scooped the to-do list off the table, stuck it in her apron pocket and snagged her borrowed coat from the hook in the mudroom.

"That's going to be too hot, Rachel...though no doubt it will be perfect tomorrow." Ida hurried back to her room and returned with a tattered jacket. "This old jacket will be better. I use it when I'm working outside sometimes."

The sleeves were too long, the garment nearly reached to her knees and she could have wrapped it around herself twice. Instead of pointing out those things, Rachel thanked her, glanced in the small mirror in the bathroom to be sure her *kapp* was on straight and hurried out to the barn.

Caleb's eyes widened when he saw her. "She gave you that to wear?"

"It's a little big."

"It belonged to my *grossdaddi*. It's one of the few things of his that she kept."

"Oh."

Caleb shook his head, as if he didn't stand a chance of ever understanding the ways of women. He'd already hooked the smaller buggy horse up to an open wagon, and he motioned for her to climb aboard.

Once she was settled beside him, he took off for the far southeast side of the property.

"The list says we're to bring back cedar limbs, pinecones if we can find any, fall leaves, cattails and a small bale of hay."

"*Ya.* It cheers her to make a holiday display that she leaves by the door."

"I thought you Montgomery Amish were conservative." She didn't mean to needle him, but somehow the words popped out of her mouth before she fully considered how they would sound.

"Oh, you won't be finding a Christmas tree in our homes, that's for certain."

"Presents?"

"Simple, homemade things." He glanced at her curiously. "You don't remember any of this?"

"Not really. It's as if...as if there's simply a hole where my memories used to be. When I try hard to remember, when I actively focus on it, the headaches return."

Caleb nodded as if that made sense. "Best not focus on it, then."

"Easier said than done."

But Caleb apparently didn't hear that. He'd pulled the wagon to a stop at the edge of a stand of trees, and now spoke to the horse, set the brake and climbed out of the wagon. As an afterthought he reached into the back of the wagon and pulled out a handsaw and a basket.

He handed Rachel the basket and motioned toward the stand of trees.

She didn't speak for a moment, then simply followed him, though she wondered where they were going. When they reached the middle of the grove, she understood. It was as if someone had carved out a spot—a secret garden of sorts. The area was cleared of trees, though she could only just see the bright blue sky above if she stood exactly in the middle. The trees surrounding them—cedar and pine and oak and birch—created a canopy that allowed the light to sift through.

"This is beautiful," she said.

"One of *Mamm*'s favorite places. Toward the back are a couple of pine trees. If you'll look for the pinecones, I'll saw off a few cedar branches."

Rachel's anxiety slipped away under that umbrella of trees. She stopped worrying about finding a job and trying to remember her past. She breathed in deeply the scent of the pines and enjoyed the unseasonal warmness of the day. She sifted through the brown and red and copper-colored leaves, filling her basket with pinecones for Ida. She was thinking of that, of a holiday display by the front door in this Plain conservative home, when something shifted.

She saw only a flash of tan, then a copper color, and suddenly Caleb's hands were on her arms, pulling her back and urging her to be silent.

She dropped the basket. Pinecones spilled across the

leaves. She reached for them instinctively as she might have reached for a glass of water that was tipped off a table, but it was too late. Caleb's voice in her ear again urged her to move back, and she was thinking of that—of how his voice caused goose bumps to cascade down her arms—when she saw the copperhead. It slithered through the leaves, its hourglass pattern blending nearly perfectly with the foliage around it.

Her breath caught in her throat, her heartbeat accelerated and adrenaline surged through her system.

"Are you okay?"

"Ya."

"You're sure?"

"How did you…?"

"I was reaching over you to get a pine bough for *Mamm.*"

"My mind was wandering, I guess…thinking of Christmas."

"I saw it slither and…" Caleb seemed to suddenly realize that his hands were still on her arms. He took a step back. "I should have warned you."

"Nein. I may have forgotten a few things…"

"Nearly everything."

"…but I'm not stupid. I know that snakes sometimes come out on winter days—especially warm winter days and if their den is close to a sunny spot."

Rachel shivered, realizing how close she'd been to it. Surely it wouldn't have struck her, but it might have…if it had felt threatened, and she had been rooting around in its winter home.

She stepped closer to Caleb. *"Danki."*

"For what?"

"For saving me…again."

And there it was, that thing that had been between them since they'd first met, since five days earlier when Caleb had found her collapsed in the middle of the road. Gratitude swelled in her heart that he had saved her, and she realized the source for some of the friction between them.

She'd always considered herself to be someone who didn't need saving.

She'd always been fiercely independent.

She wasn't sure how she knew that about herself when she didn't even know her own last name, but it felt right. Her stubbornness, her unwillingness to accept help, was all tied up in how she had ended up in this small community in southwest Indiana.

Two terrible, life-changing situations. She could have died the first time, been injured the second. She hadn't been because Caleb had been there—both times.

A pained expression crossed Caleb's face.

"You're uncomfortable with that, aren't you?"

"With what?" He picked up a stick, squatted and pushed it around the area where she'd been collecting pinecones, apparently checking for any additional snakes.

"You're uncomfortable with saving me, that's what." She laughed out loud—part nervousness and part relief. It wasn't that Caleb hated her, it was that he was what the romance books would call a reluctant hero. "You're not responsible for me, you know."

"What's that supposed to mean?"

"Some cultures believe that if you save someone's life, then you're responsible for them from that point on."

"I've never heard that before."

"It makes a certain sense. If you'd saved a horse or a dog, then you'd take it home and care for it. Right?"

"Maybe."

She kneeled beside him in the leaves, certain that he'd scared any other snakes away. "But I'm not a horse or a dog."

He purposely scooted a little to the left, away from her.

"I'm a woman."

"Uh-huh."

"But that doesn't mean you're responsible for me, Caleb." She reached out and pushed him, catching him unaware. Losing his balance, he plopped into the leaves and looked at her as if she'd lost what was left of her mind.

And yet that felt right, too—the teasing and the laughter.

Instead of explaining the thoughts that were tumbling through her mind, she resumed picking up the pinecones, this time humming as she did so.

Caleb didn't know what had come over Rachel.

He'd nearly had a heart attack when he'd seen the copperhead slithering inches from her hand, and then he'd reacted on instinct, pulling her away and urging her to be quiet.

Which she had, at first, but when she had realized what had happened, she'd looked up at him with such gratitude that Caleb had felt like he was drowning in her warm brown eyes. And then she'd begun talking about saving people and responsibility. While he was still trying to follow her train of thought, she'd begun to laugh.

He didn't have a clue as to why women acted the

way they did, and he vowed—not for the first time—
to give up trying.

"Do we have enough items?" Rachel had shed the
jacket that was his *grossdaddi*'s and set it across the
seat of the wagon.

"Items?"

"For your *mamm*, for her decorations."

"Oh. *Ya*. I guess so." But there was one more thing on
the list that he was holding, so he helped Rachel climb
up into the wagon, jogged around to the other side and
joined her, then called out to the mare.

"Where are we going?"

"You'll see."

"Does it include snakes?"

"Nein."

"Bears?"

"No bears here that I know of."

"Maybe a hive of Africanized bees?"

He glanced over at her and found her smiling mis-
chievously.

"You're a strange person, did you know that?"

"Caleb Wittmer, what would make you say such a
thing?"

"You were nearly bitten by a venomous snake less
than ten minutes ago, and now you're making jokes?"

Rachel pulled her *kapp* strings forward and ran her
fingers up and down the length of the fabric. "I wasn't,
though, just like I didn't perish in the snow. I guess
Gotte isn't through with me yet."

"I suppose not."

Caleb had fallen into the habit of thinking of Rachel
as young and immature, but he realized now that nothing was further from the truth. It was only that some-

times she would get that faraway expression, and he would assume she was lost in childish daydreams. In other words he'd judged her and done so too harshly. That was something he'd be needing to pray about, something he'd need to ask forgiveness for.

"No time like the present," he muttered.

"What's that?"

"I was just thinking that I needed to apologize to you, and there's no time like the present." He pulled off his hat and resettled it on his head. "Not something I much enjoy doing."

"And what do you have to apologize for? Saving me?"

"*Nein.* Judging you."

Rachel waited. She didn't jump in. She didn't make it any easier for him.

"I shouldn't have offered you my advice about getting a job. I should have known that you would already be thinking about that."

She studied him a minute, and then she began to laugh.

"Something funny about that?"

"Only that I did need a little push. It's not that I wasn't going to look, but I thought I'd wake up the day after you found me or the day after that and remember everything. What was the use in looking for a job when I wouldn't be staying? Why look for employment when I'd soon have my old life back?"

"It has only been a week."

"And yet, I don't remember much more with each passing day. It doesn't look as if I'll be traipsing home anytime soon."

"I'm sorry it didn't work out that way."

"You helped me see that I need to accept my situation, as it is, until it changes."

Caleb nodded as if he agreed, but in truth he was simply relieved that she wasn't still angry with him.

Her forehead wrinkled and she stared out across him, at the field they were passing. "I did speak to the bishop."

"Ya?"

"While I was in town yesterday. He's going to help me find a job."

"That's *gut*."

"I think so, since it's true that 'Amish women work hard…at least most of them do.'"

Caleb winced to hear his own words quoted back to him, but at least she'd been listening. It was important for every member of a household to contribute to the well-being of that household. Maybe she was realizing that. He certainly didn't want to bring it up—it would only seem like he was lecturing her again. Fortunately, they were at the pond, and he could change the subject.

"This is a *gut* fishing spot in the summer." He called out to the horse to stop and set the brake on the wagon.

"I didn't know you had a pond."

"Sometimes *Mamm* packs a picnic and brings it down here on warm days." It struck him that Rachel wouldn't care about that. She almost certainly wouldn't still be here by the time summer rolled around.

"So what are we here to find? I can't remember what else is on there." She tried to snag his *mamm's* list out of his hand, but he held it out of her reach, causing her to laugh more and nearly fall into his lap. He had no idea why he was acting like a *youngie*, but it felt nice to relax and enjoy the afternoon. He hopped out of the wagon, pulled a rake and a pair of garden shears from the back of the wagon, and began walking along the edge of the pond.

"We need cattails," he said.

"Not real cattails."

"*Nein.* The kind that grow around a pond, like those." He pointed to a tall stand of bulrushes. As they moved closer to the edge of the pond, he said, "Watch where you put your feet. You wouldn't want to sink in that mud."

"Native Americans used cattails to make mats and baskets."

"Is that so?"

"*Ya*, and the head can be dipped in oil and used as a torch."

Caleb turned to stare at her quizzically.

"I have no idea how I knew that." Instead of becoming gloomy over that realization, she smiled and gestured toward the tall weeds with brown cigar-shaped heads. "How are we supposed to reach them?"

Caleb held up the rake.

"Ah."

Rachel was happy to point out the tallest, prettiest cattails, as she continued to regale him with trivia.

The lower parts of the leaves could be used in salads.

Young cattails could be roasted.

Pollen of the cattail could be added to pancakes.

"Maybe you were a botanist before."

"*Ya*, because there are a lot of female Amish botanists."

The banter between them felt light and comfortable. The afternoon was warm, and it was hard for Caleb to wrap his mind around the fact that earlier that week she might have perished in the snow, but it was true. Indiana weather was like that—fickle.

What if he hadn't been mending that particular section of fence on Monday as she walked down the road?

What if she'd arrived at that spot an hour later, after he'd already gone?

For the first time since that fateful morning, Caleb was grateful that he had found her, that *Gotte* had brought Rachel into their lives. She might not be there for long. Regardless of what his friends Gabriel and Beth thought, he was neither jealous of her presence nor interested in her in a romantic way.

But perhaps they could be friends, for as long as she was there. A month or a year from now, he'd look back and laugh at the strange woman who had plopped into their lives.

As they finished pulling the cattails from around the pond, he kept thinking of the way her arms had felt under his hands, of the look in her eyes as she'd gazed up at him, then at the snake, and then back at him. It was as if the defensive Rachel, the one that made him feel like a cat rubbed the wrong way, had vanished, and instead he'd found himself staring at a woman he hadn't met yet.

He continued to steal glances at her as they loaded their items on the wagon, then he directed the horse back toward the house.

"You can quit looking at me that way."

"Which way?"

"As if I might disappear before your eyes."

"You gave me a scare, I won't deny it."

"My brother was bitten by a copperhead once." She didn't seem to realize she was remembering. A smile wreathed her face, and she held her head back, basking in the warmth of the sun. "He said it hurt worse than the time that he broke his leg. He didn't want to go to the doctor, but *Mamm* insisted. The doctor said it was probably a juvenile snake, considering the bite marks. Ethan said if that was a juvenile he never wanted to cross a full-grown adult. Did you know that the length of their fangs is directly proportional to the length of the snake? So the longer—"

"Rachel."

"Ya?"

"You just said your *bruder*'s name."

"I did?"

"Ethan." They repeated it together.

They rode in silence, until Caleb pulled the mare to a stop beside the front porch. "Another piece of the puzzle."

"Lots of folks named Ethan," she said, staring up at him again, looking at him as if he'd hung the moon.

He pulled on the collar of his work shirt, which felt suddenly tight. They were one step closer to finding Rachel's family. One step closer to his life returning to normal. He couldn't fathom why that didn't feel as good as he had imagined it would.

Rachel wasn't too surprised when Caleb hurried away, claiming he'd remembered work to do in the barn. She helped Ida to unload the hay bales, cedar branches, pinecones and cattails.

"My son ran off like a beagle chasing a jackrabbit. Any idea what that's about?"

So Rachel described their encounter with the snake and recounted how Caleb had saved her…again. She didn't mention how it had felt to have his arms around her. It was an awkward thing to say to a guy's mother, and besides, she didn't know what it meant. She didn't understand the myriad of emotions still clouding her thoughts!

Ida had plopped down into one of the rockers and was staring at her with her mouth hanging open.

"What? Did my *kapp* fall off?" Rachel reached up and checked her head. Everything seemed all right.

"I should have told you."

"About?"

"The snakes."

"Oh. That."

"Yes, that. I just sent you out there, traipsing through the woods."

"I'm not a child, Ida."

"I didn't even think to tell you to watch out for snakes. It's unseasonably warm today, and with the cold front due tonight…all of the animals are acting crazy. I saw one of the alpacas standing in the water trough."

"It's not your fault, and I wasn't hurt."

"Because of Caleb's quick thinking. I guess the Lord was watching over you, child…both times that Caleb saved you."

Rachel didn't know what to say to that, so she helped Ida set the small bales of hay in a haphazard pile beside the door and cover them with cedar branches, pinecones and leaves. The cattails propped up behind it all in old milking cans added a nice touch. It did look festive. More of an autumn display than Christmas, but at least it cheered up the place.

They'd finished with the decorations and gone inside

to work on dinner when Rachel remembered to tell Ida about her brother.

"And his name is Ethan?"

"*Ya*, I guess so."

"That's *gut*, Rachel. It's *gut* that you're starting to remember."

"But it's taking so long. I'd hoped that I would be home by Christmas." She glanced up from the potato casserole she was mixing in time to see a look of regret pass over Ida's face.

The dear woman plastered on a smile and said, "If that's your heart's desire, that is what we'll pray for—that you can be home by Christmas."

"Ida, I didn't mean to sound ungrateful."

"And you're not, only homesick I suspect."

Rachel wiped her hands on a dish towel, then walked over to Ida, stood in front of her and waited for her to raise her eyes.

"I will never forget what you've done for me. How you've taken me in and given me a home. Treated me like family."

Ida leaned forward and kissed her on the cheek, then, claiming that her allergies were bothering her, she hurried from the room. Rachel couldn't remember Ida ever mentioning allergies. She had a feeling that the tears in her eyes were caused by something else entirely, and she realized in that moment that wanting something and getting it were two entirely different things.

She wanted to be reunited with her family.

Caleb wanted her gone, or at least she'd thought that he did. Didn't he? Certainly his life had been simpler before he'd found her on the road.

But receiving what they wanted would hurt Ida. For

whatever reason, she enjoyed having Rachel around. Perhaps her life had been rather lonely, with only the one son. Perhaps she was enjoying the idea of having a daughter.

That thought caused Rachel's hands to freeze over the sliced potatoes that she was dotting with paprika. Did Ida consider her a daughter? Was that possible in less than a week?

The more she thought of it, the more certain she was. She only had to look at the jacket hung over the back of the kitchen chair, the jacket Ida had insisted she wear outside, the jacket that belonged to her father.

Rachel added pats of butter to the potatoes, sprinkled Parmesan cheese across the top and popped the dish into the oven. She would find her family, but she wouldn't forget Ida or her kindness. She vowed then and there that they would be friends for life.

Chapter Six

The cold front that had threatened Saturday arrived in the middle of the night with a foot of snow and winds strong enough to cause the shingles on the roof to rattle. Rachel woke to the smell of fresh-brewed coffee, but one look outside sent her scurrying back under the covers like a child. That was the phrase that pulled her out of bed. She wasn't a child. She was a woman and should act like one, but what she'd give for a day where she could burrow beneath the quilts, forget any chores and make the world go away.

Her mood didn't improve as she pulled on her Sunday dress and braided her hair.

What was she doing here?

When would she remember who she was?

Why wasn't her family looking for her?

By the time she made it to the kitchen, she felt as if the day had already knocked her down. It didn't help that the morning had dawned cloudy and dreary. The landscape outside the window was colorless—snow on empty fields, a gray sky, a vast horizon.

None of it looked familiar to her.

Why should that still surprise her? She'd known she didn't belong here from the moment she'd opened her eyes on Ida's couch. The fun she'd had yesterday had been a distraction from her situation, nothing more.

"This will help." Ida pushed a mug of steaming coffee into her hands, but she didn't ask any questions.

That was one thing Rachel appreciated about Ida—she didn't push.

Caleb, on the other hand, had no trouble sticking his nose into her business as they all sat down to eat.

"You're awfully quiet, Rachel."

"I've nothing to say."

"Did you sleep badly?"

She didn't bother answering him. Why admit that she'd tossed and turned most of the night? She knew that the circles under her eyes were testament to her sleeplessness. So why did he have to ask?

John focused on his meal, and Ida sent her the occasional sympathetic look.

Rachel pushed the food around on her plate and sipped her coffee.

When Ida stood up to clear off the breakfast dishes, Rachel jumped up to help her, but Ida placed a hand on her shoulder and said, "Take some time for yourself, Rachel. There are only a few dishes. I can take care of them."

So she went to the living room and sat in the rocker closest to the banked fire. Though she was facing away from the kitchen, she still heard every whispered word. Unfortunately, she had excellent hearing. She had always been able to make out the slightest whisper. There! Another thing she knew about herself. Maybe she could advertise for a lost daughter with exceptional hearing.

"What's with her this morning?"

"Perhaps she's simply sad."

"Because she can't remember?"

"Of course because she can't remember."

Rachel couldn't make out the next statement as Ida was running water in the sink, but when she turned off the faucet, the last of her and Caleb's conversation came in loud and clear.

"Seems to me she needs to move on."

"Easy for you to say, son. You know who you are."

"Rachel knows who she is, she simply doesn't know who she was."

"Our past figures into who we become."

"I suppose."

"Perhaps you could go a little easy on her."

"What did I do?"

"I'm just saying that a little compassion goes a long way."

"The women in this house are awfully sensitive if I'm in trouble for asking how she slept."

"Why don't you go and help your *dat* with the buggy?"

"Great idea."

Another moment passed before the back door slammed, and she knew Caleb had left the kitchen. She should go in there now and thank Ida for standing up for her. She couldn't find the energy, though, so instead she sat there, staring at the coals of the fire and wondering how she was going to endure the day of worship and fellowship.

Perhaps that was what she was dreading—church. Sundays had always been a bright spot for her. She loved the hymns, seeing her friends and resting for the day. She loved being with her family. Tears slipped down her cheeks, but she quickly brushed them away. She shouldn't wallow in this. She'd decided yesterday that she would be more positive.

But deciding on an attitude and actually maintaining that attitude were two different things entirely.

Their service was held in Amos's barn, but Rachel's mood only worsened throughout the morning. She didn't remember any of the names of the ladies she had met earlier in the week. The songs were familiar, but she stumbled over the words. The preaching might have been what she needed to hear, but she seemed to hear it from a great distance. The text was something from the Book of Numbers, something about Balaam and a donkey and *Gotte*'s messenger. She heard the words from the sermon but couldn't connect them to anything, and she couldn't remember when they were supposed to stand or sit or kneel.

She was always just a fraction of a second behind everyone else.

Her every move seemed to scream that she didn't belong here.

By the time the service ended, she was pressing her fingertips into her temples trying to still the pounding in her head, and Ida insisted that she rest while the other women set out the luncheon. They were meeting in Bishop Amos's barn, and Ida suggested that she go to the house and find a dark room for a few minutes. Instead Rachel walked out of the barn's main room, down an adjacent section of the building, and ended up stopping in front of the last stall, where she found a half-dozen goats curled up around one another. She went into the stall, latched the door and sat down in the hay.

Which was where Bishop Amos found her, one goat in her lap, another leaning against her shoulder and a third chewing on her *kapp* strings.

"Tough morning." He said it as a fact instead of a question. Perhaps that was why she didn't take offense as she had with Caleb.

Amos shooed a goat out of a crate, turned it over and sat on it. The young goat settled at his feet, and Amos reached forward to rub it gently between the ears.

"Many folks don't understand goats."

Rachel glanced at him in surprise. She'd expected him to want to talk about her situation. She'd dreaded it actually. But goats…now, there was a safe topic.

"I love how soft their ears are." The little guy she was holding looked up at her. She reached for its ear and rubbed it between her thumb and forefinger. The goat butted her hand as if to tell her not to stop. The goats all had long white ears, and black marks high on their foreheads. Their coats were a chocolate brown. "They're such sweet animals."

"Indeed. Did you know that one doe can produce ninety quarts of fresh milk a month?"

"That's a lot of milk."

"It is, but here's the thing—a farmer can't have just one doe."

"Why's that?"

"It would get lonely."

"Would it stop producing milk?"

"Most likely it would. You see, goats are social animals. They need each other."

Rachel had been tracing the pattern of brown and white on the goat nearest her.

"A goat will die if it's left alone. It'll quit eating and just—" he snapped his fingers "—lose its will to live."

"I'm not a goat."

"And you're not alone." Amos smiled at her as he gently pulled the hem of his pants leg out of a kid's mouth.

She remembered that now—a young goat was called a kid. The kid scampered to the other side of the stall and began head-butting another kid approximately the same size.

"But it can feel as if you're alone sometimes, and loneliness is a heavy burden. I understand that first-hand."

Something about his tone of voice convinced Rachel that he was speaking from personal experience. Instead of explaining, he changed the subject.

"I found a couple of jobs for you."

"A couple?"

He pulled a folded sheet of paper from his pocket and handed it to her. "Often what we first try doesn't succeed, so I wanted you to have more than one choice."

She opened the sheet and stared down at it. "Thank you so much."

He waved away her thanks. "At the bottom is the name of the counselor your doctor recommended—the same one you spoke with briefly at the hospital."

"Oh, I don't know if I can..."

"Afford it? Surely you remember that we take care of such things." His smile grew, and he stood and brushed hay from his pants, then stuck his thumbs under his suspenders. "*Ya.* The cost is already taken care of. I'm not saying that you have to go or even that you should go, only that you can if you'd like to."

Without pausing to think if it was proper, Rachel jumped up and threw herself into his arms. *"Danki."*

Amos smelled of soap and hay and some blend of tobacco. She'd seen him tap a pipe against the palm of his hand a time or two, but she'd never seen him actually light it. She stood there in his arms, remembering the scent and feel of her own grandfather.

Amos patted her on the back, but he didn't say anything. She wondered if she'd overstepped her bounds, if she'd done something inappropriate, but then she pulled back and saw the twinkle in his eyes.

"You remind me of my granddaughter—same sweet spirit." He walked to the half door of the stall, stepped to the other side and latched it. "You know, Rachel, *Gotte* made everything for a reason. Donkeys, goats, even people each have a special purpose. You'll find the reason that *Gotte* made you. You'll find where you belong."

She sat back down and stared at the stall's door for a long time. How had he known to say the words that she needed to hear? *You'll find where you belong.*

If she was to be honest, that was her biggest fear—never finding her place.

Could she remember if she tried harder?

Was it possible to force memories to the front of your mind?

Or was her brain permanently damaged?

All she knew for certain was that it was the most important thing she had to do—more important than finding a job or learning to crochet again. She needed to know where she belonged. Regardless what the doctor had said, she wasn't sure she ever would regain her memories. She glanced again at the paper, at the name of the counselor she'd spoken with briefly at the hospital. Amish generally didn't see a physician unless something of a serious nature was wrong, and she didn't know anyone who had ever been to a counselor. Why would they pay someone to listen to them talk? They had big families and neighbors and community.

But Rachel didn't have any of those things—not really. So maybe for her, a counselor would be a good idea. There was always a possibility that it wouldn't do a bit of good at all, but, oh, how she wanted to believe that it might.

Caleb had tried not to stare at Rachel during the service, but she was seated two rows ahead of him and to the left—on the women's side, of course. He hadn't been staring at her so much as looking in her direction. She'd kept her head down through most of the service. She'd thumbed away tears several times. She'd seemed lost when they'd stood to sing or kneeled to pray.

He did not understand her moods at all.

Yesterday, when they'd been out gathering things for his mother, her mood had been quite chipper. Then when he'd pulled her away from the snake, she'd looked at him with pure gratitude. He'd thought she was going to throw her arms around his neck. That idea caused his palms to sweat as if he'd been chopping wood for an hour. In many ways, she scared him more than a copperhead snake did. Now, why was that?

She hadn't been in the serving line with the other women, and he didn't see her eating, but toward the end of the meal he saw Bishop Amos walk back into the main room from the stall area. A few minutes after that, several children dashed back where he had been, and then almost immediately after that, Rachel came out.

Instead of eating, she grabbed a cup of water and sat down at a far table.

"Go and talk to her," Gabriel said.

"*Ya.* Go and invite her to sit with us." Beth was cradling their sleeping baby in her left arm and eating with her right.

"Who?"

"You know who," they both said.

"Who said I want to talk to her?"

"Your face." Gabriel grinned at him as he picked up another chicken leg from his plate. "Now go over there."

When Gabriel and Beth started laughing, Caleb stood up in disgust. "You two are acting *narrisch.* Maybe you need to go for a walk or something."

But he wasn't actually angry with his best friend or his best friend's wife. He just felt…out of sorts. Their laughter actually eased the knot of tension in his stomach. His friends helped to remind him that life wasn't so serious.

Why did he constantly forget that?

He'd stood up and was walking toward the dessert table, but he was thinking of that, of how he should attempt to be more lighthearted, when he practically collided with Rachel.

She let out a startled "oh." He put up his hands to try to stop his momentum, and the cup of water sloshed over the front of both of them.

"There should be some dish towels behind the table."

He didn't ask how she knew that. It seemed that Rachel remembered things best when she wasn't trying to remember them. He followed her over to the now empty serving line. She pawed around in a box behind the table and finally came up with two dish towels.

"I'm glad it was water and not milk or coffee," she said.

"I'm glad it was only half-full."

His statement caused her to laugh and that caused him to laugh, and suddenly he was reminded of Gabriel and Beth.

"Say, would you like to come over and sit with me and my friends?"

She shrugged as if it didn't matter to her where she sat, but she followed him back to the table. On the way, he snagged two different desserts and sat them down in front of them, and said, "Take your pick."

Rachel stared at the desserts as if she couldn't decide, and Caleb was afraid he'd ushered in another emotional moment, but then a smile pulled at the corner of her lips and she said, "Give me a choice, and I'll always pick chocolate. I may not know my name, but I remember that."

"Smart woman," Gabriel proclaimed.

Beth started talking about the merits of dark chocolate over regular chocolate. Rachel told them about the goats in the back stall.

"So you're that kind of girl, huh?" Caleb wiggled his eyebrows. "You know, the kind that goes and sits with the goats during a party."

"*Ya.* I'm shy all right. At least I think I am."

Gabriel was about to respond to that when the baby began to fuss, and Beth claimed she needed to go and feed him.

"Want to come with me? If you haven't been in

Amos's house, you should. He makes cuckoo clocks and has them everywhere. It's amazing."

The girls bundled up in their coats and then walked out into the wintry day, leaving Caleb staring at the dessert that Rachel hadn't eaten and his own empty plate.

"You've got it bad, buddy."

"Got what?" He pulled her plate toward him and stabbed his fork into the chocolate pie. Not that he was hungry, but it was chocolate pie. It would be a shame to see it tossed because Rachel forgot to eat it. *Who forgets to eat a piece of pie?*

"See, that's what I'm talking about. You ask a question, but then your mind wanders before I can answer it."

"How do you know that?"

"Because I know you."

"*Ya*, okay. Maybe. I've been a little distracted lately."

"A little? You practically bowled Rachel over when you went up to the dessert table."

"I was trying to think how to approach her."

"Approach her?"

"*Ya.*"

"She's not a wild horse, buddy."

"Good analogy."

"I wasn't making an analogy, and I haven't heard that word since we were in eighth-grade English class."

"She resembles a wild horse in a lot of ways—"

"Who does?"

"Rachel." Caleb pointed his fork at him. "Now whose mind is wandering?"

Gabriel raised his hands in surrender. "So this wild-horse thing. What did you mean by that?"

"Think of it. A wild horse doesn't initially know who to trust."

"Do you think Rachel doesn't trust you?"

"I think she's still scared, skittish even."

"Go on."

"Wild horses are unpredictable."

"Because they're scared, and they're wild."

"Exactly. So we need to prove ourselves trustworthy."

"We?"

"Then she'll relax, and then she'll remember who she is."

"Is that what the doctor said?"

"After that, she can go home." Caleb scraped up the last bit of chocolate crumbs into a pile, but he didn't bother eating them. Instead he stared at them, as if the answers he sought were there, amid the pile of dough and chocolate and cream.

"Is that what you want?"

"I have no idea, Gabriel." He stood and gathered up the plates. "But when I do, I'll let you know."

As he walked toward the buckets where he needed to put his dishes, he paused to look out the barn's window. Beth and Rachel were stepping up onto Amos's porch, walking close together, bundled against the cold. She didn't look skittish, not around Beth, but she certainly acted that way around him.

Why was that?

Why did he make her nervous?

And what could he do to help her feel at home and safe?

"Do you like babies?" Beth asked. Simon had fallen asleep after eating and was making little baby sounds.

His mouth formed a small o, and his long eyelashes lay softly against his skin.

"Who doesn't like babies?"

"My little *schweschder*." Beth smiled and set the chair to rocking. "She says they only eat, poop and sleep."

"She might have a point." Rachel glanced around the bishop's guest room. The living room had been full of cuckoo clocks, but the room they were in had only one—a clock shaped like a schoolhouse, with a small owl that popped out on the quarter hour. "I like them— at least I think I do. Babies are small and sweet and easy to please."

"Indeed."

"Tell me about you and Gabriel."

"Not much to tell. We grew up together, stepped out together when we were old enough and then married."

"So you always knew he was the one?"

"Actually that took a little convincing. Gabriel was a perfect boyfriend—always bringing me flowers or chocolate or taking me to a movie."

"Sounds like he was intent on wooing you."

Beth shrugged. She was about the same age as Rachel, but plump, with a round face and a ready smile. "I guess. Truth is, Gabriel liked to play, and he liked having me around to go with him. When it was time to settle down? He wasn't so sure about that."

"What changed his mind?"

"I told him that I wanted to marry and start a family. I said if he didn't, that was fine, but it might be time for me to step out with someone else."

"You said that to him?"

Beth grinned, her head bobbing up and down.

"Would you have…stepped out with someone else?"

"*Ya.* I wasn't going to wait until I was an old maid. Gabriel would have been happy betting his extra money on buggy races…"

"And buying you flowers."

"That, too. He might have carried on that way for years. My point is that he saw no need to stop being a boy, but I was bored with those things. I wanted a home and a baby." She kissed the top of Simon's head, and the baby popped the corner of his fist into his mouth and began sucking on it.

"I don't know what I want," Rachel admitted. "I feel…restless, I suppose."

"Of course you do. You're still trying to figure out who you are. Probably Gabriel was, too—before we decided to marry."

"But the difference is he had his friends and family to help him figure that out. He had you."

"You have *frienden* here, Rachel. Whether you realize it or not."

Rachel noticed that Beth didn't say this flippantly, and waited for Rachel to look up at her, to see how serious she was, to nod in agreement.

"Now, tell me about Caleb." Rachel raised the baby to settle against her breast and rubbed his back in soft, slow circles.

"What about him?"

"He seems smitten."

"With whom?" She'd never even heard Caleb mention a girl, other than the one who had dumped him for being old-fashioned.

"With you, silly. Tell me you haven't noticed."

At first, she stared at Beth, her mouth open and heat

rising in her cheeks, but then she began to laugh. The owl poked out of the cuckoo clock, chiming the quarter hour and causing her to laugh even harder, which caused Beth to join her.

"I don't know what we're laughing about." Beth dabbed at tears that were leaking out of her eyes. "But it feels *gut* to do so."

"We're laughing at the thought of Caleb being interested in me...in, you know, that way."

"So you don't think he is?" Now Beth was wrapping a blanket around Simon, tucking it up under his legs and resettling him in the crook of her arm.

"*Nein.* I think he can't wait to be rid of me."

"Really?"

"I aggravate him all the time."

"You do?"

"He corrects everything about me—my hair, my clothes, even the fact that I haven't found a job yet."

"You've only been here a week."

"Exactly."

"Do you want a job?"

"I don't know. Maybe. It might help with this restless feeling if I was doing something useful. It might help me remember who I am...or was."

"How do you plan to find one?"

Rachel reached into her pocket and pulled out the sheet of paper Amos had handed her. She stared down at it a moment and then passed it to Beth.

"Bishop Amos wrote this?"

"*Ya.* How'd you know?"

"He has a funny way of making his *t*'s. Always has." She tapped the sheet of paper. "This is a *gut* list."

"A quilt shop, a bakery, a restaurant and a school."

"Which would you like to work at?"

"I've no idea."

"Of the four, I personally would pick the quilt shop. Katherine, she's demanding but fair."

Rachel chewed on her bottom lip a minute. Finally, she said, "I suppose I could give it a try."

"Have you given any thought to seeing this doctor?"

"*Nein*. I mean, I have thought about it, but I haven't made up my mind. Seems a little…drastic."

"Could help, though. Several of the people I went to school with have been to see her—you wouldn't be her first Amish patient."

"Did they have memory problems, too?"

"*Nein*. One of the girls was an older teenager and she struggled with eating too little, another miscarried a baby the first year she was married—had real trouble moving on from that, which is understandable. The man who went to her, he blamed himself for his parents' dying in a buggy accident."

"My problems seem kind of small compared to those."

"They're not small when you're the one dealing with them every day."

"That's true, though I imagine Caleb will think it's a waste of the church's money."

"Caleb isn't as harsh as you make him sound. Maybe he comes across that way because he's intimidated by you."

"Me?" Rachel's voice rose in a squeak.

"I think that Caleb is somewhat afraid of women, but he must like you. After all, he saved you—twice."

"Anyone would have done that, I think. It's not like he could have left me lying in the snow."

"I heard that when he saved you from the snake, that he was quite shook up."

"That only happened yesterday. How did you—"

"Everyone's talking about it. You know how it is with the Amish grapevine. Or maybe you don't remember that part." Beth glanced up at the clock, which was about to cuckoo again. She stood and began gathering her things. "Here's something you should remember about Caleb…"

Rachel was pulling on her coat, but she stopped, her arm midway into the sleeve, at the seriousness in Beth's voice.

"It's not my place to share the details, but Caleb was hurt by the two girls he tried to date."

"He told me a little about that."

Beth's eyebrows rose in surprise, but she didn't comment on that. "Since then, well, it's been almost a year…"

"That long?"

"Caleb hasn't appeared interested in putting his heart on the line again. I think, that at our age, if you're hurt from something once, you shy away from it. But if you're hurt twice? It can spoil your outlook for a long time."

"He's rather young to be deciding he wants to be a confirmed bachelor."

"Except maybe it's not something you decide. Maybe it's just something that kind of becomes a habit."

"I guess."

"Anyway. Trust me—he's interested."

"In…"

"In you, silly."

"But he doesn't even know me, not really. I don't even know me."

They were walking to the door of the guest room, and Beth stopped, reached out and put a hand on Rachel's arm. "Maybe who you are isn't just your memories. I know they're important, and I know that you want yours back. I don't blame you."

She brushed at the sleeve of Rachel's coat, knocking off some imaginary lint. "But who you really are? That's your heart and how you perceive things and how you treat people. It's not just your experiences."

"So what am I to do? Forget about remembering?"

"Nein." Beth's voice softened, and she glanced down at the babe in her arms. "But maybe you're not just trying to remember for yourself. Maybe the real reason to remember is that people love and miss you—the people back home, wherever home is. I'm sure they're very worried."

"And Caleb?"

"I'd say sit back and enjoy your time together. Who knows. Maybe he'll start bringing you chocolate and taking you to *Englisch* movies."

Which was such a ludicrous thought that Rachel began to laugh as they walked back out into the snowy Sunday afternoon.

Chapter Seven

By the time they made it back home after the Sunday afternoon meal, Caleb had resolved in his mind to be kinder to Rachel. He didn't really think he'd been unkind, but perhaps he had been harsh. It certainly wasn't his place to judge her clothing or how soon she found a job. He couldn't begin to imagine what she was going through, and although he thought she should *get over it*, he couldn't honestly say that it would be easy for him if he'd forgotten everyone and everything.

The talk with Gabriel had helped.

Rachel needed to feel safe, to trust them, and then she'd remember. Once she remembered, they could return her to her home, like a lost puppy that people put up posters for in town. Had Rachel's family put up posters for her? Were they even looking for her?

He and his *dat* completed a few chores that had to be done, even on a Sunday, and then his *mamm* served a simple dinner. Afterward they all sat in the house's main room, the fire throwing out heat and a soft glow, lanterns lit against the winter darkness outside, a north wind rattling the windows. Caleb was staring at *The*

Budget, which he'd already read and so provided very little entertainment, when he saw a posting that read:

> Lost donkey, gray-colored with one white ear and one black, northwest side of Shipshewana, last seen on County Road 265. Bruno was like a pet to our family. Please call the phone shack if you've seen him.

The article ended with a phone number. He read it again, and suddenly it felt like a light bulb had gone off over his head. Of course Rachel's family was looking for her. Only, they didn't know where to look. How did you look for an Amish person that was lost? Caleb could think of only a few ways.

You could drive around, which no doubt they had done.

You could ask your neighbors, but news traveled fast in any Amish community, and if they'd known anything, her family would have been told about it within the first twenty-four hours.

You could notify the police, but most Amish families—even the more liberal ones—were hesitant to involve local authorities unless they were sure something terrible had happened. Bishops usually coordinated any communication between families and local police, and Amos was already in contact with law enforcement, as well as area bishops.

He glanced over at Rachel, who had her Bible open on her lap but was staring out the window. What if she'd been having problems at home? Maybe they didn't think she was hurt or in danger. Maybe they were trying to give her time and space. If that was the case, then eventually, like the family who missed their donkey, they would put out an appeal for information.

They might even put a notice in *The Budget*.

Scribes submitted letters for each community, and the paper was published once a week. It contained national as well as local news. It contained letters from Mennonite and Amish communities. This was how he could help Rachel. He could pore over the letters every week, looking for any mention of a beautiful young woman with a slight smattering of freckles.

He nearly slapped his forehead. He'd had this very conversation with Rachel once before. He'd promised her they'd scour the paper looking for anything that might reference a lost woman, but somehow in the business of the day-to-day workings of a farm, he'd forgotten about that promise.

He stared down at the paper he was holding. It couldn't possibly have news of Rachel's disappearance. Scribes would have penned the letters two weeks ago and mailed them to the national office, then they would have been typeset and printed. The next edition was the earliest he could expect to find anything about a girl that had gone missing a week ago.

He slapped the newspaper shut, causing his *dat* to glance up from the *Farmers' Almanac*, and his *mamm* to look up from her crochet work. Some communities frowned upon needlework on Sundays, but his *mamm* long ago insisted that if it was enjoyable and relaxing, then it wasn't work. If it wasn't work, it was permitted.

"It's been a long time since I won a game of checkers."

"Because your *mamm* and I won't play anymore. You always win." John stretched and said, "I'm too tired to get throttled on a checkerboard."

His *mamm* shook her head. "You won't talk me into it, either. I'm enjoying what I'm doing, *danki* very much."

Rachel must have been listening, because she finally turned to look at him when the room grew quiet.

"Me? I don't even know if I know how to play."

"One way to find out." Caleb wiggled his eyebrows. "If you dare."

She started laughing then, which was something he hadn't heard from her very often.

Forty-five minutes later, she'd won her third game and Caleb's *mamm* had decided they all needed coffee and dessert. Throughout the game he'd caught Rachel studying him, as if she was trying to figure something out. When he called her on it, she shrugged and turned her attention back to the checkerboard. It wasn't until they were seated around the table, enjoying apple-crumb cake and sipping decaffeinated coffee, that she admitted what was on her mind.

"I'd like to go into town tomorrow, to try working at the quilt shop. If that's okay with everyone."

"Of course," Caleb's *dat* said.

"I think you'll love working for Katherine." His mom stood to refill their coffee cups. "And maybe it will help you remember something."

"I wasn't sure how I would get there, though. You only have the two buggies and—"

"Don't worry about that," Caleb's *dat* said. "You can take the older mare and leave us with Stormy. I don't have any reason to go to town tomorrow."

Which might have aggravated Caleb the day before—his *dat* just handing off the buggy and mare to Rachel—but not tonight. Tonight he was optimistic. He was still picturing Rachel as a wild horse that needed settling, a lost donkey that needed to be found. Look at her now. She was smiling and thanking his parents, and then looking at him questioningly.

So he plopped a large forkful of apple-crumb cake into his mouth, sat back and smiled at her. She smiled back, though there was some hesitancy there.

She would learn to trust him. He was certain of it.

Then she'd begin to remember, and then she'd go home.

Wild horse or not, she belonged back with her people. The least he could do would be to help make that happen.

Rachel's morning wasn't going so well. The owner of the quilt shop, Katherine, had been kind enough. Amos had spoken with her the Friday before, and she seemed pleased when Rachel showed up at her shop thirty minutes before opening on Monday morning. No, the problem wasn't her new boss. The problem was that she couldn't remember a thing about fabric, quilting or running a cash register.

"Let me help you with that," Katherine said. Her boss was older, gray-haired and plump. She was also Mennonite, which usually worked out well for Amish employees. She understood their ways and was patient when they needed a day off to help a family member.

Katherine ran the customer's credit card through, handed the woman a special ten-percent-off card that she kept on the shelf under the register and said, "Sorry for the trouble."

When the *Englisch* woman had walked out the door, Katherine turned to Rachel and said, "It's okay. You can't expect to remember everything right away. I shouldn't have left you on the register."

She was kind enough not to point out that they'd already tried allowing Rachel to cut fabric and that hadn't gone well at all. How hard could it be to measure and cut a yard of fabric? But it seemed the process was beyond her.

"I don't even remember if I used to work in a quilt shop."

"It's a pretty standard register, so if you worked in any shop, you probably used something similar. There are a lot of different types of transactions, though, and it takes most employees a while to master all of them."

It didn't seem to Rachel that there were so many things to master in checking out a customer—cash, credit or debit? But her mind went blank when she tried to remember which buttons to push on the cash register.

She reached up and rubbed her right temple.

"Headache?"

"A little."

"Go to the break room and have a cup of tea. After that, you can work on putting together some of the quilting kits. We're selling a lot of those to *Englischers* for Christmas gifts."

Rachel nodded, but the last thing she wanted to do was work on quilting kits. Katherine had shown her how to assemble them earlier in the morning, but she had trouble reading the pattern instructions and many of the pieces were quite small.

She wanted this job to work, though, so instead of questioning her next assignment, she went to the break room, made herself a cup of herbal tea and was staring at the employee bulletin board when her co-worker, Melinda, walked up. She was thin and beautiful and impossibly young, probably under twenty.

"Planning to go on a skiing trip?"

"Huh?"

"You're staring a hole in that poster." Melinda tapped the Swiss Valley Ski poster.

"Something about it looks familiar, but I don't know why."

"Want to go up there this weekend?"

"All the way in Michigan?"

"Six hours by bus. We leave early in the morning, get there by noon and ski all day. Sometimes we hire a driver and share the cost."

"I don't think I know how to ski."

"You'd enjoy it," Melinda assured her. "And when you get on the skis, it might all come back, just like riding a bicycle."

Which was a spectacularly bad example, as Rachel had no idea if she could even ride a bicycle.

Why couldn't she remember anything?

Why did life have to be so hard at every turn?

She blinked away tears and said, "I'll think about it."

After she rinsed her mug out in the sink, she walked into the back workroom. It was a cheery area with windows along one wall and felt design boards on the other three.

She walked to the quilt kit bin and picked up a Happy New Year pattern and large Ziploc bag. Then she walked over to the fabric stack, pulled out the bolts of fabric she'd need, carried them to the cutting center and began to measure and cut.

Twenty minutes later, Katherine came in to check on her.

"How are you doing?"

"*Gut*. I've finished one and am starting another."

Katherine picked up the Ziploc full of fabric and frowned. "You're working on the New Year kit?"

"Ya."

"But you've used Christmas fabric."

"Oh."

Katherine sighed as she pulled out the fabric. "We'll have to put this in our scraps bin now."

"I'm—I'm sorry."

Her boss looked at her with eyes filled with sympathy, which only made Rachel feel worse. "Maybe you're pushing too hard. Maybe you need to give this some time."

"I like working, though."

"I know you do, and we like having you here, but, Rachel… I can't afford to lose customers because you take ten minutes to check them out. And this fabric? It's very expensive, and now it's wasted."

"It's only that I couldn't remember what batik meant and—"

Katherine smiled at her and patted her arm. "Why don't you go on home today? Talk to Ida and John. I think it would be better if we wait, maybe another month or so, and then try again."

"You mean I'm fired?"

"Not fired." Katherine shook her head so that her gray bob of hair swung back and forth. "Let's call it an extended leave of absence."

But Rachel didn't want a leave of absence. She wanted things to be normal again. She retrieved her purse from her locker and walked toward the front of the shop. Katherine stopped her at the door and pushed an envelope into her hands. "Your payment for working this morning—and don't even try to give it back to me."

Rachel nodded, muttered *"danki"* and stuck the envelope into her purse. This was bad. She wanted to be useful. She wanted to earn money to help Ida and John. She wanted to help pay for her food and any future medical bills. She couldn't just mooch off their family forever.

Caleb had been studying *The Budget* and then staring at her for over an hour the night before. She could see in his eyes that he was trying to think of how to return her to where she belonged. She was like a lost envelope with Return to Sender stamped across the front—only, no one knew who her sender was. Everyone was waiting for her to fully recover from the accident, but she wasn't getting any better.

Her mood plunged even lower as she climbed into the buggy and pulled out onto the road. At least she remembered how to drive a buggy. She stopped at the light and looked left and that was when she saw the sign for Dr. Jan Michie, Psychologist. Dr. Michie was the person Amos had recommended, the woman she'd spoken to briefly at the hospital. Even Beth had said the woman was a good doctor. Rachel had been clinging to the hope that she would improve on her own.

She wasn't improving, though.

So she tugged on the mare's reins and pulled into the doctor's parking lot, set the brake on the buggy and picked up her purse.

She wasn't helpless. There were things she could do to hurry her recovery along, and seeing a doctor was one of them. She'd do whatever Dr. Michie suggested, because she would find her lost memories. Then she'd be whole again, she would find her family and life would be exactly as it had been before.

Caleb saw Rachel turn into the doctor's parking lot. He pulled up beside her as she was getting out of her buggy. Reaching over and opening the passenger door of his buggy, he called out, "Going to the doctor?"

"Maybe. I mean, *ya.* I am."

"Do you have a minute?"

"I suppose."

"Then come in out of the cold. Tell me about your morning."

Rachel glanced toward the front door of the doctor's office, turned back to Caleb and finally smiled. "All right. It's not like I have an appointment."

She stepped up into the buggy and shut the door.

He only had a small heater in the front of the buggy, but it had been running full blast and the interior was reasonably warm.

"So why are you going to the doctor…if you don't have an appointment?"

Rachel cornered herself in the buggy and looked directly at him. Caleb suddenly realized that she was quite different from the two women he had stepped out with. They'd been young girls, unsure of their heart or mind. It had hurt his pride when they'd dropped him for someone else. In truth, it had devastated him and sent his self-confidence into a tailspin, but he could see now that those relationships weren't meant to be. When he was ready to step out again, and he wasn't interested at all at the moment, but when he was, it would be with someone like Rachel. Someone more mature, more serious, but still able to laugh at the ups and downs of life.

She took her time, weighed her words and listened. Had she been this way before her accident, or was it because she was out of her environment?

Finally, she sighed and glanced back toward the quilt shop. "You know I worked at Katherine's this morning."

"And it made you ill?"

"Nein." She smiled at his joke. "It didn't go very well. I couldn't quite catch on…"

"Catch on?"

"Remember how to do things."

"What kind of things?"

"Run the register, cut fabric, sew."

"You've forgotten all of those things?"

"Apparently."

"I'm sorry, Rachel. This must be very hard for you."

"It is." She squeezed her eyes shut and pulled in a deep breath. When she looked at him again, she seemed to have found some inner calm. "I don't mind not remembering how to sew. I don't even mind being a terrible employee at the quilting shop. It's only frustrating to know that I must have been good at something before, but I have no idea what that thing was."

He nodded, remembering the time he'd tried working in a nearby furniture factory. They'd been in the middle of a long drought, and his parents had needed the money. It was a terrible idea, and he hadn't been good at it at all. That—not being good at something—had taught him to appreciate the work that he was able to do well.

"You'll find what you're good at. The quilt shop wasn't the only place on Bishop Amos's list."

"I would like to find a job that would help me to pay my way." She scrubbed a hand over her face. "Whatever happened to me—whether it was an accident or something else—has made me realize some things."

"Such as?"

"It's important to be useful each day, to be able to contribute in some way. I have a feeling that before… that maybe I was dissatisfied a lot, that I wanted more

their community before making a decision of this magnitude? Their *Ordnung* plainly said they should remain separate, that they shouldn't take up *Englisch* ways. It seemed to him that running to a doctor when you wanted to talk was doing just that. Unfortunately, from the expression on Rachel's face he could tell that he'd offended her again. "Maybe you should give it a little more time."

Her chin came up, and her eyes widened as if she couldn't quite believe he'd criticized her—again.

"This recovery isn't happening on its own, so it's time that I did something proactive. If I don't, this could take years, and I don't want to wait that long." Her defensiveness dissolved as suddenly as it had appeared. She reached across and patted his arm. "I'm glad you happened by."

"You are?"

"*Ya.* Talking to you helps, Caleb."

"Helps how?"

"Helps to clear my thinking. Saying it out loud stops the loop of thoughts going on in my mind." She opened the door, hopped out of the buggy and then leaned back inside. "I enjoyed beating you at checkers last night."

"I'd rather win now and then."

"See you around."

"I guess you will." He'd meant it as a joke, something to lighten her mood, but Rachel cocked her head as if it was one more puzzle she had to figure out.

Finally, she smiled, waved and strode off to the front door of the doctor's office.

The *Englisch* doctor.

The one that was going to help her recover her memories.

* * *

Rachel walked into the doctor's office. It was pleasantly decorated—the walls were painted a soft warm yellow and decorated with pictures of pastures, fields and sunrises. She gave her name to the receptionist and explained that she didn't have an appointment.

"Should I come back? I don't know what I was thinking just stopping by."

"Let me check with Dr. Michie first."

She turned back toward the waiting area and sat in one of the comfy chairs. The table in front of her had a few magazines, and to the right of her was a built-in cabinet with a coffee machine and all sorts of coffee and tea. Soft music played in the background. A small Christmas tree sat in a corner on the far side of the room. It was decorated with ornaments made by children—that was obvious from the overabundance of glue used on them and the fact that glitter had fallen onto the tree skirt.

Overall, not a bad place to wait.

She made herself a cup of herbal tea and picked up a magazine. Five minutes later, Dr. Michie poked her head through the door into the waiting room.

"Rachel? Would you like to come on back? You can bring your drink with you."

"Danki."

She followed the doctor back to her office. She'd met her only once, in the hospital. Jan Michie was slightly taller than her, not thin but not overweight, either, and had brown hair cut in a short shag. She wore glasses from a chain and was dressed as she had been before— neutral-covered slacks and a knit top. The most calming feature about her was her demeanor. She always seemed relaxed and unhurried.

"Thank you for seeing me, Dr. Michie."

"Call me Jan, please. I was hoping I'd hear from you. How are you doing?"

"Okay, but not great. Obviously. If I was great, I wouldn't be here."

"Tell me about that."

"Are you sure you have time?"

"Yes. I had a few open hours, and I was catching up on paperwork."

"But if you need to..."

Jan shook her head and sat back in her chair, sipping from a blue coffee mug. When she saw Rachel staring at the mug, she turned it so she could read the logo better. It said, I'm a Psychiatrist. What's Your Superpower?

"Cute," Rachel said.

"From my nephew."

The doctor didn't rush her or ask more questions, which was exactly what Rachel needed. She glanced around the office, which was also nicely decorated, and then stared out the window. Someone had filled up a bird feeder, and a variety of winter birds she couldn't name were hopping around enjoying the buffet.

Had she enjoyed bird-watching before?

What kind of person had she been?

Was her family looking for her?

Instead of asking any of those questions, Rachel blurted out, "Caleb doesn't think I should be here."

"Is that why you came to see me? To talk about Caleb?"

"Yes and no. I'm tired of not remembering. I want my life back. I want me back."

"We talked about this in the hospital. Do you remember that conversation?"

"I do. You said sometimes it takes weeks or months or even years."

"How's your memory of more recent events?"

"Gut."

"And you've kept your follow-up doctor appointments?"

"The first is later this week, but I feel as fit as a horse." She tapped her head. "The thing is that I don't want to wait any longer—not months and certainly not years. I want to do whatever I need to do to regain my memories."

Jan sat back, folded her arms and studied her for a moment. Then she opened a file that had been sitting on her desk and read through a few pages of notes—probably from when they'd visited in the hospital. Finally, she shut the file and said, "Okay. Then let's talk about what you can do to hurry this process along."

"Wunderbaar."

"I'm not guaranteeing anything."

"Of course not."

"But at this point, I'm pretty sure anything we do won't hurt your recovery."

"And it might help."

"Exactly." Jan paused, steepled her fingers and finally asked, "And you're sure that you want to remember? Because sometimes when we delve into our past, we find things weren't as rosy as we'd have liked them to be."

"I don't understand."

"Sometimes not remembering is a way of protecting yourself. Perhaps you had an incident that was painful physically or emotionally, and so your mind doesn't want to remember because it's traumatic to do so. Sometimes what we uncover isn't what we would have hoped to find."

"I hadn't really thought of that. I guess it's possible, though unlikely."

"Abuse happens in all types of families. I'm sure you realize the Amish aren't exempt."

"But I don't feel abused."

Jan waited.

"I appreciate you warning me, but I think not knowing is worse than anything we might discover—*gut* or bad makes no difference. I just want to know. I want to know who I was before."

They spent a few minutes talking about what might help her recover her memories—spending thirty minutes each morning and each evening just sitting, resting, allowing her mind to relax.

"Pretend you're floating in the ocean."

"Don't know if I've ever done that."

"What I mean is just relax. Don't try to remember. Don't do anything. Some people have trouble being still and quiet, but it can be a very healing thing. Find a special place where you can go and do this."

"Will a stall in a barn do?"

"Perfectly, as long as there are no distractions."

"Okay."

"And remember to write in a journal. Would you like me to give you one or can you purchase one?"

"I have one that I've been writing in." Rachel shared with her the short list of things she'd remembered thus far—her name, that she had a brother named Ethan, wearing sunglasses, knowing about alpaca wool and that she was twenty-five.

"Great. Be sure and continue adding to that list. Nothing is too small to include. In fact, it would be good to make daily entries, and bring it with you for your next appointment."

"What do I write about…if I don't have anything to add to my memory list?"

"Absolutely anything. Don't try to force your thoughts in any one direction. If it comes into your mind during your journaling time, jot it down."

"Sounds easy enough."

"You had a poetry book with you when Caleb found you, correct?"

"*Ya.*"

"Read through it, not forcefully, not intent on making yourself remember. Putting more pressure on your mind will only cause it to skitter in another direction."

"Like when you're trying to remember the words to a hymn and just can't."

"Exactly, but when you quit thinking about it…"

"Usually when I'm doing laundry."

"Then the words come." Jan tapped her pen against her desk. "The poetry book is one of the only physical clues we have to your past, and I think it's an important one. I'd like you to spend a few minutes each day reading it, but do so as if it were a letter from an old friend—something you enjoy revisiting again."

Rachel began to feel optimistic. Dr. Michie made her sound less like a freak and more like a person with a treatable condition.

"If you have time and a buggy, drive around a little. Just pick a direction and drive. We can't really guess what will stir your memories."

"I can do that."

"Be sure and make a note in the journal if anything

looks familiar or causes you to experience a strong reaction."

"I will."

"Also if you have any dreams that leave you with intense feelings, jot those down, too."

Rachel nodded and stood when Jan glanced at her watch.

The doctor plucked a business card from her desk drawer and handed it to her. "If you need to talk, call me." Then she stood and walked her into the reception area. She asked her receptionist to make Rachel an appointment for the next week.

"One more thing." She put a hand on Rachel's shoulder. "If there's anything that you find you enjoy doing—then do that thing. If you like it, then your mind is signaling to you that it's a safe activity, and the opposite is true, too. If something seems terribly hard—"

"Like cutting fabric." She'd shared her attempt at working across the street.

"Yes, like cutting fabric—if it seems hard, if it brings on the headaches, simply stop. Don't push. If it seems like something you'd enjoy, though, allow yourself to do it without understanding why."

"I can't imagine what that will be."

"You'll know when you see it."

Rachel walked back out into the weak afternoon sun. The day was as dreary as it had been before. The shop that she wouldn't be working at still sat across the street, its parking lot now half-full of customers. Nothing had really changed, but for a reason she couldn't put her thumb on, and for the first time since she'd woken in Montgomery, Indiana, Rachel felt hopeful.

There was a small general store on the way back to

the Wittmer farm. She stopped and went inside, unsure what she was looking for or why she was bothering to shop when she had such a small amount of money to her name. Then she remembered what Jan had said, about doing something she enjoyed. She'd been surprised to find thirty dollars in the envelope from the quilt shop. She didn't think she'd earned that much, but apparently she had. While she could give the money to Ida to help pay for her food, she had a feeling Ida would rather she follow the doctor's directions.

So she walked up and down the aisles, pausing in front of the paperback novels, the cookbooks, even the coloring books. None looked particularly interesting to her. She turned down the next aisle and saw a large display of yarn. Beside that was a variety of crochet needles, books and knitting needles. She reached forward, ran her fingers down a pair of 5.5-m knitting needles and almost laughed. She picked the package up, turned it over and over, and finally slipped it into her basket. Next she chose a package of variegated yarn—beautiful blues melding into one another, from sky blue to navy. It would make a lovely scarf for Ida, and she knew just the pattern to use. She could almost see the directions in her mind— a stockinette stitch that produced a nice woven look.

She checked the items in her basket to be sure she had what she needed, added another skein of the yarn and then walked to the register to pay for everything. She couldn't have said if she really knew how to knit, but it felt like she knew, and after all…the doctor had told her to follow her instincts. For now, her instincts were leading her toward a hot mug of tea and a knitting session.

Chapter Eight

Caleb had been studying Rachel all through dinner and even afterward as she set to work with her new knitting needles and yarn. She'd apparently begun the project earlier in the afternoon—after losing her job, visiting the doctor and going by the general store. She'd been busy. Whatever she was knitting already stretched across her lap. How much of the yarn had she bought? It was a medley of blues—quite appropriate. He couldn't fault her there, not that he was looking for a reason to find fault. He just didn't understand her moods, and he was worried about this doctor situation.

He'd tried to catch her eye a few times, but she'd been completely focused on counting her stitches. Twice now she'd shushed him.

His *mamm* had laughed and said, "That's why I was never very good at knitting—you have to count."

Rachel had nodded in agreement as she continued mumbling, "Thirty-seven, thirty-eight, thirty-nine…"

He waited for her to reach the end of a row and tug again on the ball of yarn, and then he jumped in with the first thing that came to mind. "I could use some help in the barn brushing down the horses."

She stopped, midstitch, and stared at him. "Now?"

"Sure. Now's a *gut* time."

She bent forward to peer out the window at the pitch-black night. The cloud cover was so heavy that no stars or moonlight shone through, but she shrugged and said, "*Ya.* I could help with that, I guess."

Caleb noticed his parents exchange a glance, but he chose to ignore that. The year before, his *mamm* had spent many an hour trying her best at matchmaking and dropping none-too-subtle hints about *grandkinner.* She'd finally given up sometime in the last six months, but he knew that sparkle in her eye meant she was considering meddling. He shook his head once, definitively. She only smiled and raised her eyebrows as if to say "I have no idea what you mean."

"*Gut* to see you *youngies* taking responsibility for our animals." His *dat* peered at them over the top of *The Budget.* "Those alpacas—I'm not exactly sure what to do with them."

"Mostly they enjoy attention," Rachel said, as if she'd been raising alpacas all of her life.

For all Caleb knew, she had been.

"I'll put a kettle of water on to boil, and we can have tea and some of those leftover cinnamon rolls when you all are done." His *mamm* added, with a distinctive twinkle in her eye, "But don't hurry on our account."

Caleb rubbed at the muscle just over his left shoulder and waited for Rachel to shrug into her coat.

They walked out to the barn in silence, the wind at their back causing them to walk closer together—shoulder to shoulder—as a barricade against the cold.

When they stepped into the barn, the smells of hay and animals and wood surrounded him. He watched Rachel as she walked around the main room, studying the tools and projects and sacks of feed. Finally, she turned to him and said, "You and your *dat* keep a clean barn."

"Of course."

"Not all Amish do."

"You remember that?"

She shrugged, unprovoked by his intrusiveness. She'd been quieter, calmer, since going to the *Englisch* doctor…or maybe it was the knitting that had settled her nerves. "I'm not sure what I remember, but I do know this is especially clean. Can't say I'm surprised, since you're so…"

"So what?" He didn't want to care what Rachel thought about him, but he braced himself for her criticism as if it was a dart she was about to hurl his way.

"Industrious. That's the word I'm looking for."

"Never been called that before. Thick-headed, stubborn—"

"Old-fashioned. *Ya*, I know. But what I mean is that you seem to like what you do out here, and it shows. It's not about doing things the old way…though plainly you do." She picked up a handheld seed broadcaster, studied it a minute and placed it back in its cubby. "People can be old-fashioned and messy. This place looks as clean as a veterinarian's hospital."

Had she worked for a veterinarian?

Everything she said, he wondered if it was a piece of the puzzle of Rachel, but maybe he was reading too much into things. Maybe he was afraid it was all going to come together at once, and she'd be whisked away. That was what he wanted, for her to be returned home, but he hoped it would happen slowly so that he could get used to the idea. He should already be used to it, since he spent an inordinate amount of time thinking about it—about her.

"So why did you want me to come out here?"

"I told you—"

"To brush down the horses at seven thirty in the evening. *Ya*, I heard you."

"Could be a guy just likes a little help with the work. Plus I get a little restless, especially on winter nights. We've been sitting in that house since five o'clock."

She only smiled wider, and he knew that he wasn't fooling her. She didn't call him on it, but plainly she knew that he'd brought her out here to talk about the doctor. She'd said nothing about it at dinner, which meant she'd talked to his *mamm* earlier. While he tried to figure out how to broach the subject, they might as well brush down the animals.

The alpacas usually stayed outside, even in the evening. They had a lean-to with a roof and a wall against the northern wind. They could also come into the barn through the southern stalls, where he left the outer doors open. He'd been doing that the last three nights, and each morning he'd arrived to find them bedded down inside. Apparently they knew a good deal when they saw one, and since his *dat* had only the two buggy horses, they had several unused stalls.

He handed her a brush and pointed to the nearest stall, and together they walked in and began brushing down Ginger, their older mare. Rachel didn't ask any questions about how to use the brush or where to begin on the animal. She talked to it softly and then began stroking it from the top of its head and down its neck. The animal apparently liked what she was doing. When she stopped to move her *kapp* strings out of the way, the mare nudged her hand to encourage her to keep brushing.

He thought Rachel looked especially pretty in the glow of the lantern. He was suddenly glad that she had fallen into their lives. He was already starting to think of events in terms of "before Rachel" or "after Rachel," as if she was some sort of dividing line in his life. She was certainly unlike any of the girls he had stepped out with. Rachel had a mind of her own, even if she couldn't remember her name. She had strong opinions, but she was willing to listen to others—that was rare in a person. And though she seemed to struggle with her moods, he couldn't know if that was because of the frustration of her situation or something more. She seemed to always push through. She seemed to always end up with that same small knowing smile she was wearing now.

A bead of sweat broke out along his hairline, and he felt as if he could hear the rush of ocean waves in his ears. What did that mean?

Was he falling for her?

Did he have…romantic feelings for Rachel?

That would be ridiculous. Why would he even entertain pursuing a relationship with her? It wasn't like she was staying here. It wasn't like they had a chance to build a life together. Then again, how much control did one have over whom they fell in love with?

He dropped the brush, bent to pick it up and stumbled as he was standing back up.

She looked at him quizzically but didn't say anything.

He couldn't be in love with Rachel. He just couldn't. He liked things done the old way, while she was eager to embrace change. He was quiet and steady—his mood was the same nearly every day. She was smiling and chatty one moment, quiet and droopy the next. He lived in Montgomery, Indiana, and they had no idea where she lived. He couldn't even speak to her *dat* about courting her because they didn't know who her father was.

It was with those thoughts whirling in his head that he swallowed, began brushing the other side of the mare and broached the subject he'd wanted to talk about since she had come home earlier that afternoon.

Rachel thought Caleb was acting a bit strangely— staring at her one moment, then dropping things, then stumbling, and then blushing when he saw she'd noticed. If she didn't know better, she'd ask him if he'd been sipping the wine that many Amish households kept for special occasions.

She didn't, though.

The thought of Caleb Wittmer drinking a glass of wine almost caused her to laugh out loud. So instead of quizzing him about his odd behavior, she waited for him to begin the interrogation that she knew was coming. She certainly wasn't going to make it any easier for him, but she did feel a bit sympathetic that he was grappling with it so.

Finally, he began brushing the mare with strong sure strokes and jumped in.

"I don't understand why you have to see an *Englisch* doctor."

"We already talked about this in the buggy."

"I know we did, but explain it to me. I really do want to understand."

"And I want to understand why you're so dead set against it."

"Good, let's have a conversation. You start."

"All right. I want to see Dr. Michie, who is an *Englisch* doctor, because I want to get well. And we don't have any Amish doctors."

"We may not have doctors, but we have people in our community who can help you."

"Like who?" Rachel crossed her arms, her aggravation building. She should have known that he would have a better idea. Caleb always thought he knew the answer to things. Though she'd promised herself that she would be more patient with him after all Beth had told her, that was proving more difficult than she'd thought it would be.

They'd had that nice moment in the buggy earlier in the day—he'd seemed almost kind then. No doubt he was a kind person, but sometimes his certainty that he knew the best answer for every question got in the way.

If only he wasn't so aggravating and pushy, she might actually enjoy being around him.

He was studying her now as if she was a child and he needed to think how to persuade her without causing a tantrum. She did not have tantrums! She might have strong opinions, but there was nothing wrong with that.

"You were about to suggest people in your community who could help me find my memories."

"Let me think," he said.

"Uh-huh. I'm waiting."

They both continued brushing down the mare. It had been a long day for Rachel with too many ups and downs. She was embarrassed that she'd lost her job at the quilt shop on the first day she'd shown up, but she was also optimistic after seeing Dr. Michie. Now Caleb was ruining even that.

Ginger moved closer, so she continued brushing her mane. It was amazing how much animals enjoyed human attention.

"Many people in our community see a chiropractor," Caleb pointed out.

"I don't have a sore back!"

"I'm just saying that there are…" He paused, his eyes going up and to the right as he tried to think of another word.

"More traditional?"

"That's it. There are more traditional ways to address, uh, health issues."

"This is a *mental* health issue."

"Maybe it is. Maybe it isn't. Your brain was apparently bruised—sounds physical to me."

She shook her head in exasperation.

"We have midwives."

"Not having a baby."

"And we have an herbalist." He snapped his fingers. "That's it. You could go see Doreen."

"An herbalist?"

"*Ya.* She's very *gut.* Lots of people say so."

"Have you ever seen her yourself?"

"*Nein.*"

"Have your parents?"

"Not that I can remember."

"But you want me to go and see her."

"*Ya.*"

"I thought herbalists helped people who had digestive issues or maybe trouble sleeping." She started to add "people who were depressed," but she wasn't ready to admit she had that problem. Maybe she did, but maybe her feelings were a natural reaction to what had happened. If her moods were a side effect of her amnesia, would that still be considered depression? She'd have to ask Dr. Michie the next time she saw her.

"I have another appointment with Dr. Michie next week."

"Oh."

She could practically hear him snap his mouth shut, as he no doubt tried to stop the suggestion that was about to come out. Maybe he did realize how irritating he was—points in his favor. She felt her aggravation with him soften.

She felt her resolve wobble.

"If you think it's a *gut* idea to see this Doreen, I suppose I could give it a try." She didn't want to see an herbalist, but it might be worth it to please Caleb. He suddenly looked so relieved, almost as if it was already Christmas morning. "No idea where she is or what I'll say to her."

"I'll take you."

Caleb glanced away when she stared up at him.

"Now, why would you do that?"

"Just trying to help."

Ginger again nudged her hand, encouraging her to keep brushing, and Rachel laughed—whether at herself, Caleb or the mare, she couldn't have said.

"I don't have anything to do tomorrow, since I lost my job. The manager at the restaurant didn't want to see me until Wednesday."

"Tomorrow afternoon, then. I'll take you over to Doreen's."

"It's a date!" Rachel wanted to take back the word as soon as she said it, but Caleb was looking at her as if she'd just told him there was an alien standing behind him. It really was comical.

Did he think she wanted a date with him? He looked seriously stumped, so she shook her head, patted the mare one last time and moved over to Stormy's stall. There was no point in trying to clear up misunderstandings as far as Caleb Wittmer was concerned. She'd tried that before, and she usually ended up digging a deeper hole.

She started working on Stormy, who really was a beautiful animal. His coat was a deep black, and he was delighted to receive the attention. After twenty minutes, Caleb admitted they should go back inside, that his *mamm* probably had the tea ready. They both knew that brushing the horses had been an excuse for them to have a little privacy.

As they walked back toward the house, staying close together against the north wind that seemed to cut right through her coat, Rachel felt her mood plummet again. She'd felt almost content for a few moments, working on the scarf for Ida. The yarn and knitting needles had seemed to move effortlessly between her fingers. But now her emotions were churning again. She'd agreed to see this Doreen, but she didn't hold much hope that any herb would help her to remember. It was quite possible that Dr. Michie's suggestions wouldn't, either.

All she knew was that she wanted to go home, to be where she belonged, and she was willing to try just about anything to achieve that.

Caleb barely said a word through their evening snack and as he made his way to bed. Did Rachel think they were going on a date?

How did he get himself into these messes?

And why, as Gabriel had pointed out, was he so skittish around her? He should be happy that she'd agreed to see the herbalist, though why he'd suggested Doreen he couldn't have said. All he knew was that Rachel didn't need to see that *Englisch* doctor. Amish folks did see doctors—sure they did—for things like broken legs or deep cuts or rotten teeth. They didn't see a doctor for their feelings, and this Michie woman... It wasn't as if she was a specialist in memories. There was no such thing. Was there?

He went to sleep Monday night feeling like he'd done a good thing steering Rachel back toward the Amish way. He wanted her to get well, wanted it as much as she did, but he didn't think paying a woman to talk to her for an hour was the answer. If she needed to talk to someone, she could talk to him. He wouldn't charge her a thing!

The next morning again dawned dark and gray. They were certainly having a string of gloomy days. Saturday's sunshine and the episode with the snake seemed like it had happened weeks or months ago. Unfortunately Rachel's mood seemed to mirror the weather. He was learning that mornings were the hardest for her. She seemed to perk up by afternoon. And cloudy days? They were the worst.

His *mamm* and *dat* seemed a little surprised that Caleb had suggested Doreen, but they didn't offer an opinion. Instead they shared a look. He'd seen unspoken words pass between them as long as he could remember, and he still didn't understand how they did that. His *mamm* sipped her coffee and said, "I wish I could tag along, but I promised to go over and help Rebekah finish up a quilt for the new grandbaby she's expecting. Both her girls are due with their first about the same time, and she's in quite a tizzy over getting ready for them."

So it was that after lunch he found himself pulling the buggy up to the front door and waiting for Rachel. He didn't have to wait long, and when she did come out, she at least looked perkier than she had that morning.

"Feeling better?" he asked.

"Who said I was feeling bad?"

"Doesn't take a genius to see."

"I guess."

"Want to talk about it?"

"Nein."

"Fair enough."

They traveled in an uncomfortable silence. Caleb didn't remember where Doreen lived, but his *mamm* had written down instructions on the back of an envelope. Fortunately, it was only a few miles away, so he wouldn't have to endure Rachel's silence for very long.

He needn't have worried.

By the time they were on the main road, she was chatting about red birds and Beth's baby and the knitting she'd started the evening before.

"Going better than the crochet work, huh?"

"You noticed that?"

"Looked like a cat had taken hold of your yarn ball."

"Think you could do better?"

"Nein. I wasn't saying that at all." He couldn't help smiling, though. The world felt right when Rachel teased him. When she was quiet and sad, he felt as if he had a stone in the pit of his stomach.

"Tell me about this Doreen," she said.

"Not much to tell."

"Really?"

"She's older." He thought she might have celebrated her ninetieth birthday, but he decided not to bring that up.

"Amish?"

"*Nein.* She's Mennonite." Some folks thought she was struggling with dementia, but he was sure that was an exaggeration. Though he had heard that she wore a knitted cap with pom-poms even during the heat of summer.

They pulled up to a tiny little home that was probably surrounded by gardens, but snow covered the entire property now. No one had shoveled the walk. He supposed she didn't get out much, being as old as she was. There was no sign near the lawn advertising her herbs, but the name Penner was stenciled on the mailbox.

"Her name is Doreen Penner," he explained as he pulled the buggy to a stop.

"I wonder where she keeps her plants in the winter."

But they didn't have to wonder for long. Doreen answered the door, with a striped cat in her arms and a rather large parrot sitting on her shoulder. "I don't know you, so I guess you're here to see me about some herbs. Come in. Come in."

"Come in," squawked the bird.

As Caleb had feared, she was wearing a knitted cap done in a striped purple pattern with a large pom-pom on the top, but her clothing was even stranger than her headwear. She wore a denim dress embroidered with cats chasing yarn, cats chasing butterflies, even cats chasing children. The dress reached to the floor, and her outfit was rounded out with pink bunny slippers and a pink sweater that was unraveling. The cat stared at them briefly, yawned and then began to lick Doreen's hand.

Rachel shot Caleb a look that told him there would

be a reckoning coming as soon as they left the house. She thanked Doreen politely and stepped inside.

The home looked to be four rooms—a living room with windows that faced the street, a dining room to the left of that. Beyond, Caleb could just make out a kitchen, and the bedroom must have been to the right of the back room.

Every conceivable surface was covered with plants. They were crowded onto tabletops and windowsills, lined along the floor beneath windows and even crowded on top of stacks of books. Doreen placed the cat on the floor, and it immediately disappeared between a large aloe vera plant and a cactus.

Who grew cactuses in Indiana?

"Come into the kitchen and tell me what type of treatment you're needing."

"Actually we just wanted to talk with you," Rachel said.

A calico cat had replaced the striped one at Doreen's feet. It walked over to Rachel and began to rub against her legs. She stooped to pet it, and Caleb could hear the beast purring from where he stood. This was a nightmare—instead of a physician's office, he'd brought Rachel to a house with an undetermined number of cats, one large bird and an old woman wearing a purple knitted cap on her head.

Caleb fought the urge to turn around and head back out to the buggy, but Rachel was already walking toward the kitchen, explaining that she'd suffered a slight concussion and amnesia.

"Is that so?"

"*Ya.* It happened a little over a week ago, as near as we can tell."

"So you're not from around here. That would explain why I don't recognize you, though I've seen your beau at barn raisings and such."

Caleb wished he could melt into the yellow linoleum floor. Rachel's beau? Had the old woman actually said that?

"Sit. Both of you, sit and talk to Doreen."

The chairs were filled with more books, some newspapers and seed packets. Caleb cleared off a place for Rachel to sit and then another for himself.

"Caleb, he found me in the snow out near his parents' farm. They took me to the hospital." Rachel put a hand at the back of her head. "I had a lump, but no other injuries."

"And you can't remember any details of your past?"

"Not at first. A few things have returned since then—the name of my *bruder*, that I wore sunglasses, a couple of childhood memories."

"How interesting." Doreen sounded delighted to be presented with such a challenge. She hobbled over to the stove and set a kettle on the burner.

Caleb glanced at Rachel in alarm. "I'm not sure we can stay long enough—"

"Nonsense. It's rude to not offer guests a cup of tea. Isn't that right, Peaches?" The bird's head and back were adorned with turquoise blue feathers, but its breast was a bright orange.

It squawked, "Tea," and then flew away to perch in the boxed windowsill amid a sea of plants.

"Macaws aren't the smartest parrots..."

"Smart bird." Peaches's head bobbed up and down when he spoke.

"African gray parrots are better at understanding and mimicking human speech, but Peaches is good company."

"Good company." The bird began to groom himself, and Caleb didn't know whether to laugh or hang his head in his hands. Who let a bird fly around their home? There wasn't a cage in sight. Doreen made a cooing sound, pulled a baby carrot from her sweater pocket and offered it to the bird, who squawked, "Carrot," and snatched it from her hand.

"Do you think you can help me?" Rachel asked.

Doreen's back was to them as she fiddled with the teakettle. Rachel glanced at Caleb, then pressed her fingers over her lips in an attempt to hold in her laughter.

"A cheerful heart is good medicine," Doreen said, pulling three cups and saucers from her cabinet. There was no place to put them on the counter, so Caleb jumped up and took them, carrying them over to the table. Doreen followed with a metal tin. Her hands shaking, she slowly opened it, dug around among the contents, pulled out three bags and placed them in the mugs. "The Good Book says that."

"Proverbs," Rachel said.

"Proverbs," squawked Peaches, though his attention had switched to a solid yellow cat. He dropped to the floor, strutted across the room to the cat, who was lying near the back door, and began to preen it.

"Yes. Now, some people think herbs are just weeds, but we know better—Peaches and I do. *Gotte* gives us everything we need. People have been using plants for medicine since Adam and Eve stepped out of the garden—after all, there were no pharmacies then."

"What kinds of things do you treat?" Rachel asked.

"Mistletoe can help with a nervous disposition or high blood pressure."

"I don't have either of those things."

"Peppermint helps with sleeplessness."

"She doesn't have trouble sleeping," Caleb said. If they didn't move this along, they'd be here all afternoon. They hadn't come for a botany lesson. In fact, he couldn't quite remember now why he'd thought this would be a good idea.

If Doreen heard him, she chose not to respond.

"Rhubarb is useful for eczema or arthritis." Her hands shook as she reached for Rachel's and covered them with her own. "Now, your situation is unusual. I would normally use ginkgo leaves for someone who is confused, but you seem mentally alert."

"*Ya*, I think I am."

"What you need, what I've put in your cup, is rosemary."

"Rosemary?" Rachel asked.

"Rosemary," Peaches squawked, flying across the room and landing on the table.

Caleb jumped backward, causing his chair to scrape against the floor. He couldn't believe he was seeing a large blue-and-orange bird on a kitchen table. Certainly, that couldn't be healthy.

At the same moment, the kettle whistled. Caleb jumped up. "I'll fetch that." He did not want to drink anything Doreen gave him. What if the parrot had been in her cabinets? What type of disease could they catch from the bird? Or the cats? He might as well eat off the barn floor.

Rachel seemed nowhere near as tense as he was. In fact, she actually seemed to be considering drinking the rosemary tea.

He filled their cups, then stood behind Doreen, telling Rachel with hand motions not to drink or eat anything. Rachel, being more than a little mischievous, smiled at him, raised the cup to her lips and nearly drained the contents in one swallow.

"That's a girl." Doreen dunked her own tea bag up and down. "I think your beau will enjoy it, as well. What was your name, young man?"

"Caleb." He shrugged back into his coat. "I just remembered somewhere we need to be."

"Need to be," the bird squawked and jumped to Doreen's shoulder, where it began to poke its beak in the woman's purple cap.

"One of the reasons I wear the cap in the house." Doreen smiled as if she'd said the most clever thing. "It's better than having my hair preened. Peaches is very affectionate."

Caleb wanted to leave—immediately.

Rachel was in much less of a hurry. She wouldn't meet his gaze, and he couldn't quite tell if she found this situation humorous, or if she was simply hiding the anger she was going to unleash on him once they were back in the buggy. Not that he would blame her.

"*Danki* for the tea, Doreen. Do we owe you anything?"

"For a cup of tea?"

Caleb had walked around the table and was pulling Rachel to her feet. She continued trying to thank Doreen. Peaches was squawking about seeds and carrots. Yet another cat had jumped into Caleb's vacated seat. He felt as if he was caught in a bad dream.

Rachel's life had been topsy-turvy since she'd opened her eyes with no memories the week before. It had been dramatic and terrible and frightening and difficult.

Today was like the cherry on someone's ice-cream sundae. She honestly didn't know whether to laugh or cry.

Caleb practically pulled her out of Doreen's house—the bird was still squawking and one of the cats tried to follow them outside, but Doreen scooped it up in her arms. Rachel glanced back to see Doreen standing in the doorway, Peaches on her shoulder, one cat in her arms and another rubbing against her legs. The dear old woman waved at them and hollered, "Come back anytime."

Which didn't seem likely.

Caleb seemed intent to get her into the buggy as quickly as possible. Even the gelding, Stormy, seemed surprised to see them back so soon. How long had they been inside Doreen's house? Fifteen minutes? Twenty at the most.

She climbed up into the buggy and pulled the buggy blanket over her lap. Caleb jumped in, called out to Stormy and took off at a speed that had the gelding tossing his head and threatening to break into a gallop.

And then it happened. All of the tension and worry and anxiety of the last week caught up with her. She sat forward and covered her face with her hands.

"I'm sorry, Rachel. I really am."

She took two deep breaths—she knew what was coming, but was powerless to stop it.

"That was one of my worst ideas ever. I'd heard that Doreen had gone a little strange, but I had no idea…" Caleb touched her shoulder. "Are you okay?"

He called to Stormy and pulled the horse over into a parking area. "Are you—are you crying? Wait…you're laughing?"

Her shoulders shook and her laughter came from a place deep inside. She laughed until she had to clasp her stomach from the ache. Tears sprang from her eyes, and every time she thought she had control of herself, she'd glance at Caleb—Caleb, who was staring at her with eyes wide and a look of disbelief on his face—and she'd dissolve into laughter again.

He waited her out and handed her a handkerchief when she seemed to be finished.

"Oh, my. I haven't laughed that hard since my sister fell in our pond trying to pull in a fish." Another puzzle piece, and she knew then, she was convinced, that there would be more until her life resembled something that she recognized. "The look on your face when Peaches jumped on the table made me wish I had an *Englisch* camera."

"Never seen anything like it." He crossed his arms as if he was still perturbed about the whole thing.

"And your pantomiming not to drink." Laughter spilled out of her again and she wiped at her eyes.

"So why did you drink it?"

"I thought that was the reason you took me there— to receive Doreen's cure."

"You did it to spite me."

"Actually it simply seemed polite, and I didn't think a little rosemary could hurt me. Seems my *mamm* used to add some to our tea when we had a headache."

"Cats all over the place, plants everywhere, that bird… It was a nightmare."

"Carrot," Rachel squawked, and then she was laughing again, only this time Caleb joined her.

She was rearranging the blanket on her lap, trying to get control of her emotions, when he reached across and placed his hand under her chin, turning her face toward him. His touch caused her stomach to do funny things, or maybe that was the burst of laughter or even the rosemary tea.

"You're something else, Rachel. You're a special woman. Did you know?"

"Because I can laugh at an old woman's attempts to lighten other people's loads?"

"Because you can find the humor even in an extremely uncomfortable situation." She had the bizarre thought that he was going to kiss her then, but instead he pulled back his hand and picked up the horse's reins.

They continued toward home, and though the clouds still pressed down, Rachel's heart felt lighter. "Parrots are known for their problem-solving abilities, and the African gray she mentioned? It's said they have the intelligence of a five-year-old but the temperament of a two-year-old."

"A two-year-old that never grows up."

"Indeed, but I suspect Peaches is a good companion for Doreen."

Caleb shifted in his seat. "Are you going to the restaurant tomorrow...to work?"

"I suppose. I really should find a job. Sitting around all day isn't helping me, though the knitting...it makes me feel calmer."

"Wasn't the schoolhouse on Amos's list?"

"*Ya.* I thought I would try it if the restaurant doesn't work out."

"Maybe you should try the schoolhouse first."

"Why? I'm not sure they really need me. Most schools have only one teacher. Amos said the teacher in your community could use an extra hand during the holidays, preparing for the school play and all. I had the feeling it was a charity position if nothing else worked out for me."

"I know Martha. She's a *gut* teacher, but she definitely has her hands full. Our schoolhouse is brimming with children. Plans are to build another and divide in the summer."

"Why do you think I should work there?"

"Because you know things."

"I know things?"

"*Ya.* Like about the parrots."

"Oh, that was just…something I remembered."

"And the snake. Remember all the things you told me about snakes?"

"Why did I know that?"

"I think maybe you were a teacher before. That would even explain the book of poetry you were carrying with you."

Rachel stared out the window at the snowy fields. Could she see herself teaching? She supposed she could. She wasn't sure she had the temperament for it—her moods were too up and down, but perhaps it had been something that she was good at.

She turned toward Caleb and studied his profile. He was a nice-looking man, and he was trying to help her. "Your last idea was terrible."

"True."

"I want to continue seeing Dr. Michie."

"Can't blame you. She probably doesn't have cats or parrots in her office."

"But I think you might be right."

"You do?"

"*Ya.* I'll go to the schoolhouse tomorrow. We'll see what Martha says."

Chapter Nine

The next week flew by for Rachel.

She saw Dr. Michie two more times. Though she was still remembering very little of her past, she was learning to cope with her current situation. She didn't mention her moods to the doctor. Frankly, she was embarrassed that she woke each day feeling as if she couldn't crawl out of bed. Once up, after she'd had coffee and eaten, her mood usually improved. If the weather was sunny, she walked to the little one-room school. If it was snowing or if the wind was blowing, Caleb or John drove her there. As far as the evenings went, some were good and some were bad. Wasn't that true for everyone?

She kept her appointment with the medical doctor who had treated her at the hospital. Dr. Gold assured her that she was healing, and reminded her that "these things take time."

Martha was easy to work with. She was a few years younger than Rachel, and she planned to marry as soon as school was out. There would be openings for two new teachers, since the board had decided to proceed with plans to build an additional schoolhouse on the far side of the district. Rachel sometimes wondered if she should apply for the job, but as Dr. Michie had told her, "Don't worry about making tomorrow's decisions today."

So she'd focused on the children and the upcoming Christmas play, and in her spare time she did those things that Dr. Michie had suggested. On the afternoons Caleb picked her up from the school, they drove in a random direction to help her look for anything familiar. A comfortable friendship developed between them and maybe something more.

Sometimes when she thought of how much she owed the good man sitting next to her in the buggy, how *Gotte* had blessed her life with the presence of him, she was certain that their friendship would develop into love. Each night she'd allow her mind to play back the events of the day—and more often than not, her thoughts focused on something Caleb had said, or the casual touch of his hand as he helped her into or out of the buggy, or the way her heart raced when she looked up from her knitting and caught him studying her. Was that love? Did she care for Caleb the way a wife cared for a husband? And did he return her feelings?

The knitting was the only thing that completely relaxed her. Because she had to focus on counting her stitches and following a pattern that she somehow remembered, she wasn't able to worry or question or think. She found that creating something that would be useful to someone else gave her a sense of satisfaction. Perhaps she had been a skilled knitter in her other life. She might never know. More and more she was coming to terms with that.

One night she'd stayed up past everyone else. The house smelled of fresh cedar and pinecones and baked desserts. Candles adorned every windowsill, and three wrapped presents in plain brown paper with midnight blue bows were arranged on the top shelf of the bookcase. Ida was in full holiday mode.

It was hard for Rachel to fathom that it was the week before Christmas. Her dreams of being home for the holidays seemed foolish now. She still didn't know where home was. She was alone in the sitting room when Caleb's *dat* wandered in claiming he was suddenly hungry and needed a small snack.

He brought back the pitcher of milk, two glasses and the coconut-cream pie that Ida had made for dinner.

"Actually I'm full, but *danki*."

"You're very welcome. Since you don't want any, maybe I'll just finish it." He smiled at her and wiggled his eyebrows, as if this would be their little secret.

Rachel continued knitting. Christmas would arrive before she knew it, and she still didn't have all the projects done she'd hoped to finish.

John ate his pie in silence, and then he sat back and stared at the fire in the potbelly stove.

"When I met Ida, I knew she was the one, but Ida... she wasn't so sure."

Rachel glanced up in surprise. John smiled weakly and then turned his attention back toward the fire.

"She wasn't being unkind, but she wanted to be sure—*absolutely sure* was the way she put it."

"That's a rare thing, to be absolutely sure of something, to be beyond-a-doubt sure."

"Indeed it is. I was persistent, and eventually she agreed to marry me."

"So it was love."

"Maybe...or maybe it became love sometime down

the road." He stood and returned his dishes to the kitchen. She heard the water running as he rinsed his plate and cup. When he walked back into the sitting room, he picked up where he'd left off—or maybe he simply said what he'd meant to say all along. "We've had a *gut* life, me and Ida. I'm glad she gave me a chance. Sometimes that is all it takes, you know—giving love a chance to grow."

He walked over and kissed her on top of the head, something that surprised Rachel as much as his words. She stayed up another hour, the knitting sitting in her lap unfinished, her eyes on the fire and her heart wondering if she was brave enough to give Caleb a chance.

Caleb was supposed to pick Rachel up the next day. He made the mistake of arriving a few minutes early. There was a literal traffic jam of buggies in the schoolyard. He should have come later, but he hadn't wanted her to start walking home. It was snowing and nearly dark outside, though the time was only four in the afternoon. A line of buggies waited to pick up children, which was quite unusual. Amish students were made of hardy stuff. They were used to walking to and from school. Next thing he knew they'd be whipping out cell phones to call their parents to come and get them.

That was a ridiculous thought, and he knew it.

Still, he didn't like change—any hint of change caused his anxiousness to rise like cream in a pail of fresh milk.

Then he walked into the classroom and saw the decorations and the children, and he knew—absolutely knew—that he should turn around and walk back out.

Too late for that, though. Rachel had spied him and was walking toward him with a strained smile on her face.

Be reverent, in spirit low, at the manger lowly. Be gen-
rous, be thoughtful." One cat tapped another on the
ead when he said "thoughtful."

"See?" Amos said. "Same words, same meaning and
elebration, only presented a little differently."

Different ought to be Rachel's middle name.

For all he knew, it was.

Rachel's head was pounding as she pulled on he
oat and followed the last child out of the schoolhouse
aleb was waiting in the buggy. He had at least turne
he heater on so that she wasn't chilled quite to the bone
ut he still had his customary grimace in place. Hadn
e been laughing this morning at breakfast? How wa
e able to irritate him so thoroughly and so complete
such a short amount of time?

The clouds seemed to press in around them ar
snow fell relentlessly. She tried to remember wh
ing felt like, but then remembering wasn't exact
strong suit lately.

hey'd driven the short distance down the road a
d into the lane to home. Suddenly she could
his sulky silence any longer.

hat have I done now?"

ave no idea what you're talking about."

course you do. You're glaring, and if you p
t down any harder over your head, you're go
e your scalp."

right. Since you asked…"

do you have to change everything?"

se me?"

are Christmas Bees not good enough for y

"What's wrong?" she asked.

"Who said anything was wrong?"

"The look on your face."

"What's that supposed to mean?"

"You're scowling."

"Am not." He plastered on a smile, but it seemed to take the strength of a giant to hold it in place, so he returned to studying the chaos in front of him.

"What are they doing?"

"Practicing for the play."

"What kind of play?"

"The Christmas play, of course."

"Doesn't look like it."

"See, that's the fun part. We took the traditional Christmas play…you know the one, Christmas Bees."

"A *gut* play, but they don't look as if they're dressed up as bees."

"They're not, that's what I was explaining. I changed it a little, and we're calling it the Christmas Cats."

She pointed at the decorations—instead of snowflakes connected one to another, there was a string of cats, paws linking them together. Some wore glasses, some were short and fat, others were tall and lanky. Each wore a sweater that bore the name of a student.

"Why did you have to change it?"

"Because the children didn't want to be bees this year," she said.

"Cats? That makes no sense. What do cats have to do with Christmas?"

"It's funny. You'll see."

"But why would you change it?"

"So the children would be interested."

"Why couldn't they be interested in bees?"

Before Rachel could answer, one of the students ran up and said, "I don't want to say this." He thrust a sheet of paper into her hands. "I want to make up my own words."

"Let's see how that works." She threw a is-the-day-over-yet gaze at Caleb, but it did nothing to ease the ache in his jaw. Why would he think it was a *gut* idea for Rachel to work at the schoolhouse? Sure, Martha had been eager to receive help during the holiday season, but he should have known that Rachel would try to change things, to encourage the children to be different, to make them less Amish.

Bishop Amos had walked in the back door. As Rachel hurried away, he approached Caleb and motioned toward two chairs, where they could sit.

"She's doing a *gut* job, *ya*?" Amos slipped a thumb under his right suspender and smiled at the children.

"I'm not so sure."

"How's that?"

"She's using cats—changing the Christmas Bees to Christmas Cats. Why would she do that?" Caleb was sure that the bishop would be as shocked as he was, and possibly even insist that she change everything back. He didn't know how they could do that before the play the next evening, but maybe if everyone pitched in.

"*Ya*, we talked about that. Very cute idea."

"Cute?"

Amos looked at him, quizzically, then broke into a smile. "Sometimes I forget how much you hate change, Caleb."

"We're Amish. Change is what we work against."

"I can see how you'd feel that way." Amos combed his fingers through his beard. "That's not completely accurate, though. All things change. Think of how early

Christians often had to worship hidden awa rooms. We no longer need to do that. We a worship as we please."

"What does that have to do with the childre play?"

"I'm only making the point that all change It's unfettered change that we avoid. Rachel ca and asked about the changes in the script b presented them to the children."

"She did? Why would you approve it?"

"It's a small change, Caleb. You'll see. I being a bee holding up a shield with a word or cats and they hold up slate boards with th chalked on it. The entire thing is quite cleve

Caleb allowed his head to sink into his l

This was a nightmare. The bishop migh yet—no one ever said that bishops were when the parents found out what their c doing, Amos would understand that Ra a huge mistake.

At that moment, the group of smal recite their lines:

Cats follow, oh, this is true.
But cats can make good things
And that, today, is what we ha

At which point, one cat fell each other over and creating a line. All of the children, or ra and meowing as they clamore down was a clever ruse to p

Caleb stared around the

Why couldn't the children cut out snowflakes for decorations? Why did you have to change it to cats?"

"Oh, Caleb…"

"Not an answer." They'd made it to the barn. He still held the reins, and Stormy waited patiently for him to jump down and open the barn door. Instead Caleb turned to look at her. "I honestly want to know."

"The children were dragging their feet, giving Martha a hard time, not wanting to participate. I don't know why. Some years… I think some years are like that."

"Which is why they're paying you to help her."

"And I did. So I changed up a few things. Now the children are excited, in case you didn't notice, and participating happily."

"Why can't they be happy with the old ways?"

"They are. They're not asking to sit on Santa's lap or put a Christmas tree in the schoolhouse."

"There is that to be thankful for."

Rachel tied the strings of her outer bonnet, picked up her school bag and purse, and reached for the door handle of the buggy. "You know, Caleb, I did check with Amos before I made any changes. I didn't know that I had to run everything by you, as well."

And then she fled into the house.

Inside was warm and cozy, and Ida met her with a hug and a smile, pushing a hot mug of tea into her hands. But for once tea didn't work. Rachel admitted to having a headache and fled to her room, where she spent the next ten minutes having a good cry. Not a very mature thing to do, but it certainly helped her to feel better.

She avoided speaking to Caleb the rest of the evening.

The next morning she left early, insisting that she

could walk the short distance to school. She came home only long enough to make a sandwich for dinner and change clothes. Then she returned to the schoolhouse, promising Ida that she'd see her there.

For some reason she wasn't a bit nervous about the play or the children or even the parents' reactions. But if she was honest, she longed for Caleb to approve of the work she'd done with the children.

She caught sight of him coming in the back door twenty minutes before the play was set to begin. The room was crowded with parents and older siblings and even a few *Englisch* neighbors. Generally everyone in an Amish community came to a schoolhouse Christmas celebration—whether they had children attending the school or not.

The Christmas program included stories, songs and, of course, the play. It was all a smashing success. The audience joined in singing a final carol, and then the students presented Martha with a gift box holding new pens, beautiful stationery, hand lotion and candles. It was obvious that every child there had a hand in contributing.

Nothing unexpected happened until Martha called up Rachel, and one of the youngest—a lad named Nathan— handed her a gift-wrapped book. "It's more poetry, because we know you like it," he said. The entire audience laughed at that as young Nathan screwed up his face when he said the word *poetry*. Rachel laughed along with them and thanked both the children and Martha for allowing her to help.

Bishop Amos had mentioned to her that Martha would like her to continue helping after the short Christmas break—like most Amish communities they took off only the day before, the day of and the day after Christmas. She supposed she would continue doing the job. The work was exhausting, but looking at the children she knew it was worth it.

Ida and John both gave her a hug and then said they were riding home with a neighbor, which seemed a bit odd to her. It also felt awkward. The last thing she wanted was to be alone with Caleb. She was surprised when he turned left out of the schoolhouse parking area instead of right.

"Have you bumped your head? Home is the other way."

"Thought maybe we'd celebrate."

"Celebrate?"

"Your play. It was very *gut*."

He glanced her way, grimaced and resettled his hat on his head. "Don't look at me so. I can admit to being wrong."

"You can?"

Now he laughed, and the sound caused the tension she'd been carrying since the day before to dissipate. "Rachel, I am sorry that I criticized your handling of the school play. Obviously you know more about children— and parents—than I do. Will you forgive me?"

A dozen memories passed through her mind then.

Caleb staring at her when she woke on Ida's couch.

Caleb standing in the door to the hospital room, looking at her as if she might perish before his eyes.

Caleb pulling her away from the snake.

Caleb attempting to protect her from a parrot and one very sweet old woman.

Those memories softened her heart and ministered to the hurting places from when he had criticized her rather harshly. But it was John's words that echoed in her mind and convinced her to accept his apology.

What was it he had said? *Sometimes that is all it takes...giving love a chance to grow.*

"That was a very nice apology."

"It was?"

"Indeed, and I do forgive you, Caleb."

"That's it?" He was smiling at her now. "I don't have to write sentences or read extra chapters?"

"Hmm... I hadn't thought about that. Maybe it would be a *gut* idea..."

He claimed her hand, pulled it toward him across the buggy seat. "I shouldn't be putting ideas in your head."

She tried to act as if it was normal for Caleb to be holding her hand. "Where are we going?"

"To celebrate your play—I said that already."

"And what is your idea of celebration?"

But she should have known he'd pick the ice-cream shop, which was open late on Fridays. Caleb loved ice cream. Of course, he chose vanilla, while she went for cherry pistachio. Their choices reflected their personalities, and maybe that was okay. Maybe it was fine that they didn't view life the same way. Maybe it took different points of view to make things work.

On the drive home, he pulled her across the seat and tucked the blanket around both of their laps. "Cold in here," he said gruffly, but his eyes said something more.

And when they'd pulled into the barn, instead of jumping out of the buggy, he turned toward her, placed his hands on both sides of her face and asked if it would be all right if he kissed her.

She nodded, unable to speak, unable to even think clearly, as she melted into the kiss.

Chapter Ten

Gabriel went into town with Caleb the next day. They were standing in line waiting to order food when he slapped Caleb on the shoulder. "Don't look so glum. So you love her?"

"I do. I love her. Don't ask me how I know that after only one kiss, but, well...I've been fighting these feelings for a while."

"It's a *gut* thing."

"It is?"

"Indeed. Trust me on this, I know."

"But what...?" Caleb's mind was spinning. He was in love with Rachel. When had that happened? How had it happened? And the worst fear of all—what would he do if she didn't feel the same?

They placed their orders and found a table.

"You know what the old folks say." Gabriel leaned forward as if he was about to share a priceless nugget of wisdom. "No dream comes true until you wake up and go to work."

"I don't think that proverb is referring to love and marriage."

"Could be, though."

"I don't see how."

"Ask her. Then you'll know how she feels."

The girl at the counter called their names, indicating their orders were ready. "I'll get that," Gabriel said.

Caleb nodded and sat there, staring at a copy of *The Budget* that had been left on the table. He pulled it toward him, barely seeing the printed words, and turned the page more out of habit than any real need to read.

He loved Rachel.

How could he not have realized that before?

How could he have been so blind?

He turned the page again and glanced up at Gabriel, who was thanking the woman at the counter and carrying the tray of coffee and sweets toward their table. He looked down at the newspaper again, seeing but not seeing it, and then his vision cleared. Words danced across his vision. *Young woman missing, age twenty-five, brown hair and freckles.*

With his pulse thrumming so loudly that it felt as if his ears were clogged, he pulled the paper closer and began to read.

It had become a habit to read *The Budget* and check for news of Rachel. At first he'd done it in the hopes that she could be returned home, like a parcel that had been left at the wrong house. Then he'd done it because he knew how much it meant to her—to find her family again. And now? Now he read the words with fear coursing through his heart.

Deborah and Clarence Yoder of Goshen, Indiana, have asked for help in locating their daughter, Rachel, who has been missing since Friday,

November 30. Rachel was last seen walking home from the neighborhood schoolhouse, where she has been an apprentice teacher for the past several months.

The Yoders explained that they did not file a missing-persons report, believing that Rachel might have traveled to a neighboring community to see extended family. As the weeks had passed, and Rachel had not been in contact, they'd become more concerned.

Rachel was described as five foot six inches, with brown hair, brown eyes, a smattering of freckles and a slender build. She recently celebrated her twenty-fifth birthday. Anyone with information was told to contact the Yoders at the phone-shack number listed at the end of the article.

"Anything interesting in there?" Gabriel set the tray down on the table and plopped into the booth across from him. "Say, you look like you've read your own obituary."

Caleb stared down at the article in *The Budget*. He couldn't believe what he was seeing. Why now? What were the odds that today of all days he would find the one thing he'd spent weeks looking for? Printed in black-and-white were the words that he'd both longed for and dreaded seeing.

Ignoring Gabriel, he pulled the paper closer and read the piece again, then he pushed it toward his best friend.

Gabriel let out a long, low whistle as he crammed a sticky bun into his mouth. He read the article between gulps of coffee and finally tossed the paper back toward Caleb. Hoping he had misread or imagined the entire thing, Caleb read the words a third time. When he noticed his hands shaking, he dropped the paper onto the table.

Gabriel sat staring at him, waiting. Finally, he crossed his arms on the table and leaned forward. Lowering his voice, he asked, "Do you think it's her?"

"Sounds like it."

"Can't be sure."

"Until we call the number."

"Or let Rachel call the number." Gabriel nudged Caleb's blueberry muffin and coffee toward him. "Eat. You look like you're going to be sick."

Could this be his Rachel? It had to be. Didn't it?

"Maybe it's not her."

"It's her." Caleb was clutching his coffee mug so hard that his knuckles had turned white. He took a swallow, hoping the caffeine would wake him up, prove that this was all just a bad dream. "The article says that this girl—this Rachel—went missing on Friday."

"And you found our Rachel on Monday."

"So where would she have been from Friday to Monday?"

Glancing around the coffee shop, he realized the answer to that question didn't matter. None of his questions were important. The only question that mattered was whether the Rachel that belonged to the Yoders and the one living in his parents' home were the same.

But then he noticed the fourth paragraph, which he'd overlooked before.

Rachel was believed to have been wearing a dark gray coat, a blue scarf, and she might have been carrying a small book of poetry.

His heart sank. He tore the article out of the paper, folded it, stuffed it into his pocket and then took another sip of the coffee. It tasted bitter, and he pushed the mug away. "I have to tell her."

"Technically you don't have to…"

Caleb pierced him with a glare.

"But you should."

"Of course I should. I love her, as you so astutely pointed out, and love doesn't keep secrets." Already he'd accepted his feelings for Rachel. After fighting them for the past three weeks, it seemed ridiculous to continue doing so. If he didn't care about her, this news wouldn't hurt so badly.

"Listen, Caleb…" Gabriel waited until Caleb met his gaze. "This doesn't mean it's the end. It only means that you're turning a corner, beginning a new chapter, walking into a fresh start."

It was with those apt analogies ringing in his ears that Caleb stood, tossed his uneaten muffin in the trash, set the coffee cup in the to-be-washed tray and headed out into a cold and blustery December afternoon.

Rachel was hard at work finishing Caleb's sweater. Since she'd discovered that she could knit—in fact, had a real talent for it—she'd moved at lightning speed making mittens and a scarf for Ida and a hat for John. All that was left was to complete Caleb's sweater. She'd fussed over which yarn to buy but settled for a variegated gray—something conservative enough that he should approve of it.

Unlike the dress she'd been wearing when he'd first found her.

That thought brought a smile to her lips.

She'd considered him to be so arrogant and stuffy—more traditional than the old men who sat in the back on Sundays and gave pointed looks to the *youngies*. Caleb wasn't like that, though. It was only that he cared deeply and worried about the future of his community— she'd learned those things for certain when he'd confronted her at the schoolhouse. The memory sent a river of warmth through her. Had he actually kissed her? What did it mean, if anything? And when were they going to talk about it, or was he going to pretend it had never happened?

But it had happened, and she understood that he'd crept around her defenses and was laying claim to her heart. At least that was how it felt. But how could she ever fall in love when she didn't even know who she was? Correction, she knew who she was now, but she didn't know who she had been. There was a difference.

"Your needles are a blur over there." Ida plopped down across from her at the table and pulled out her crochet work.

"Remember when I tried crocheting?"

"You worked that yarn into the biggest knot I had seen in quite some time."

"I couldn't get the stitches right, couldn't figure out how to hold the needle. It all felt so…wrong."

"Obviously you were a knitter before."

"And still am."

"Indeed."

A comfortable silence fell between them. It occurred to Rachel that although she'd longed to be home by Christmas, to at least know where home was, she was grateful to have this place with people who cared about her until the Lord saw fit to restore her memory.

Thinking of the Wittmer family caused her mind to drift back again to Caleb and the way he'd looked at her the night before and the kiss. It was only a kiss. She was acting like a *youngie*. She was acting starstruck and moony, when in fact she was a grown woman.

She was about to bring up the subject of beaus and kisses and love—Ida seemed to have a pretty level head regarding just about any subject—when Caleb burst through the back door.

Rachel was facing him, so she saw him skid to a stop, his mouth open as if he was about to speak. But then he snapped it shut again after he'd glanced at his *mamm*.

Ida looked over her shoulder. "Caleb. You're home."

"*Ya*. I'm home." He moved toward the coffeepot, which happened to be on the portion of kitchen counter directly behind Ida. Eyebrows arched, mouthing something Rachel couldn't understand, he motioned with his arms. He looked for all the world as if he was playing some bizarre game of charades, but she had no idea what he was trying to say. She shook her head and started to laugh.

"Am I missing something?" Ida asked, not bothering to look up from her project—which, if Rachel wasn't mistaken, was a pair of blue mittens that would match her own scarf very well.

"Only Caleb trying to tell me some secret apparently."

Caleb shook his head from side to side and held a finger up to his lips to silence her.

"Oops."

"Oops?" Ida was smiling now.

"I think it must be a Christmas secret."

"*Ya*, that's exactly what it is." Caleb clomped around the table, took the knitting from Rachel's hands and pulled her to her feet. "Maybe you could get your coat and walk with me to the barn."

"The barn, huh? Must be a pretty big secret."

"*Mamm*, we need to go on a Christmas errand. We might be gone for an hour."

"You two have fun. I have a few Christmas surprises of my own to tend to."

But Rachel's smile faded as Caleb pulled her across the yard and to the still-harnessed horse.

"Get in."

"The buggy?"

"*Ya.*"

"This isn't about Christmas?"

"*Nein.*"

Suddenly her feet wouldn't move. She felt as if cold fingers had gripped her neck. Caleb opened the door and put his hand on her elbow. His expression was somber, pained almost. What had happened in the last few hours? What could it be that he wouldn't share with his own mother?

The frigid December wind seemed to whip right through her coat, but being warm wasn't her biggest concern.

"Tell me," she whispered as she climbed up into the buggy.

He leaned forward and kissed her once—briefly, softly, and then he shut the door, jogged around the buggy and hopped in. His eyes met hers and Rachel felt as if she was falling, as if Caleb was all that stood between her and some giant wave about to sweep over them.

He pulled a page torn from *The Budget* out of his pocket. It had been folded several times, and he set it gently in her lap, pointing to an article midway down the page. As she picked up the paper, he fidgeted with the small heater in the buggy, cranking it all the way up.

"I don't understand." She stared down at the paper, trying to focus on a single line of print.

"It's your family—your real family. I think I found them."

She read the article once and then again. By the time she'd finished it the second time, tears stung her eyes and her throat felt as if it had closed up completely. She shook her head, noticed that Caleb had directed the horse away from the barn and they were moving down the lane.

"How did you find this?"

"I've been looking."

She closed her eyes and tried to settle her emotions. Caleb's hand on hers brought her back into the moment.

"At first I studied *The Budget* every night."

"You were that eager to be rid of me?"

"I thought it was what you wanted—to go home."

"It was what I wanted, and I've been watching, too…" She glanced back down at the article, noted the date at the top of the page. "This is today's paper—I haven't seen it yet."

"Then later, I suppose I continued looking in spite of how I felt."

"How you felt?"

"I was convinced that you couldn't be happy here, and that the single thing that would bring you happiness was to know where you came from, to find your old life. And who could blame you? Of course you want to be reunited with your family."

She nodded, trying to find words to express the conflicting emotions weighing on her heart—trying and failing.

He pulled into the small parking area next to the phone shack, but instead of getting out, he turned toward her and covered both of her hands with his.

"You're shaking."

"Am I?"

"Rachel, whether this is your family or not, you know you have a place here."

She didn't know what to say to that, so she leaned forward and kissed his cheek. He offered to wait in the buggy. "*Nein*. Come with me, please. I'd like you…to be with me."

It was a typical phone shack, three feet by three feet, with a counter running along one wall. On top of that counter was a push-button phone, a recording machine, a pad of paper, a pen and, of course, a jar to put your money in. A hand-printed sign read Calls Now Fifty Cents.

Caleb fetched the coins from his pocket and deposited them in the jar.

Rachel's hands were shaking too badly to punch in the number listed in the article, so Caleb did it for her. He again offered to step outside, to give her some privacy, but she pulled him back next to her and clutched his hand as the line on the other end began to ring.

A man answered on the fifth ring, and Rachel began to cry, tears running down her face like raindrops against a windowpane. "Ethan? Ethan, is that you?"

"Rachel?"

"*Ya. Ya*, it's me."

And then she collapsed onto the stool, the phone

slipping to the counter as she covered her face with her hands and began to weep.

She was aware of Caleb picking up the phone, speaking to her brother, and then he said, "*Ya.* We'll call back in ten minutes. Go and get them. *Nein.* We'll wait. We'll wait right here."

It was perhaps the longest ten minutes of her life.

Caleb put his arms around her, held her until her shivering stopped, then thumbed the tears from her cheeks.

"It's really them?" His voice was grave, and Rachel realized for the first time the effect this turn of events must be having on him.

"*Ya.* It is. That was—that was Ethan."

"Your *bruder* who was bit by the snake."

She nodded. "He's my older *bruder.* Always acted as if he had to look out for me."

"So you're remembering?"

"Some. Not everything." But suddenly she did remember... Ethan as well as her sisters—Clara and Becca and Miriam. She remembered, and she missed them so much that it felt as if her heart would burst.

"It's been ten minutes. Are you ready?"

"*Ya.* As ready as I can be."

She clutched Caleb's left hand as he punched the number in with his right, and then she was hearing her mother and father on the line and all of the fear and loss and grief melted into nothing, like snow disappearing on a sunny day.

She'd found her family.

She was going home.

Caleb felt drained as they walked out of the phone shack and toward the buggy. The day had been saturated in emotion—disbelief, realization, love and now gratefulness and joy, and beneath all of that a little fear. Only hours before, he had realized that he loved Rachel, but he couldn't ask her to stay. He understood then that he'd made up a story in his head—something along the lines of Rachel not wanting to go home, of her amnesia being the result of an unhappy home life there.

But what he'd just witnessed was the opposite of that.

He knew, without a doubt, that Rachel loved her family and that they loved her.

He knew that she was going home.

"They wanted to come and get me, to hire a driver to bring them down here and then carry us all back."

"Nearly five hours, if I remember correctly. I've only been through Goshen a time or two."

"I couldn't let them do that." She hugged her arms around herself, pulling her coat more tightly. "And tomorrow is Sunday. We don't travel on Sunday unless it's an emergency."

"Rachel—"

"It's okay. Really. Just knowing that they're there, waiting for me, that's what matters. I can take a bus on Monday."

"Christmas Eve."

"*Ya.*"

The snow had begun to fall again, leaving a fine layer on the top of her shoulders, on the borrowed coat. Night was coming, and in the remaining light he could just make out her expression—relief and joy and wistfulness.

He wanted to remember her this way, standing in the light snow, standing as if she was inside an *Englisch* snow globe. The snow falling, her cheeks rosy, her eyes studying him. It would have been a beautiful December evening, except for the breaking of his heart in two.

"Do you think I can get a bus ride on Christmas Eve? I told them I would, but do you think that will be possible? Tomorrow is the beginning of the holiday for most businesses. Do you think they'll be running?"

"Sure and certain." He attempted a confident smile as he helped her into the buggy. Once he joined her, he picked up the conversation where they'd left it. "Lots of folks going home for Christmas. The bus will leave at six o'clock Monday morning, like it always does. We should be able to—"

"We?" Her eyes widened and her mouth gaped open.

"You don't think I'm just going to put you on a bus, send you on your way and leave you in the hands of a bunch of strangers."

"I'm a grown woman, Caleb Wittmer."

"That you are," he mumbled. Forcing a smile, he said, "Rachel—"

"Yoder. My name is Rachel Yoder." It was as if she'd discovered the cure for the common cold. She clasped her hands over her mouth in what seemed like disbelief. "No wonder the bishop couldn't find who I was. Must be hundreds of Yoders in Indiana."

"Thousands."

"Tens of thousands." They both smiled at the exaggeration, but it helped to ease the tension between them.

"What I meant to say was, Rachel Yoder, if you would allow me, I'd be happy to accompany you to Goshen."

She was shaking her head before he finished. "I can't let you do that."

"Let me?"

"If you went with me on Monday, you wouldn't get back home until Christmas Day or possibly the day after. I can't let you leave your family. You're—you're all they have."

"You know my *mamm* and *dat* pretty well by now. Do you really think they'd want me to send you off on the bus all alone? You don't even have all of your memories back yet."

"My memories are returning, though. Slowly they are returning."

Caleb almost told her then—how he felt, how they should be together, that he wanted to spend the rest of his life with her. But the smile on her lips as she said those words—*slowly they are returning*—told him what he needed to know. Rachel wanted to be with her family. It would be wrong for him to stand in the way of that.

He was happy before he met Rachel, surely he could find that contentment again. Couldn't he?

Caleb plastered on a smile, called out to Stormy and set them trotting toward home. He'd do the right thing. He'd see her home, and then he'd bury any feelings that he had for her.

He was a little concerned about how he would break the news to his *mamm* and *dat*, but he needn't have worried. Rachel walked in the front door and practically flew into Ida's arms, tears running down her face as she told her about the news article and the phone call and her family. Ida assured her that everything would be fine, and John patted her on the shoulder.

For a moment everyone was talking and saying things like "*Gotte* is *gut*" and "we knew they'd find you" and "just in time for Christmas."

They all sat, and Caleb explained how he'd seen the

article while he was with Gabriel, how he didn't want to raise anyone's hopes, so he'd made up the story about a Christmas errand.

"It was a Christmas errand of sorts," his *dat* pointed out.

Ida pulled Rachel into the kitchen, set her at the table and put on a kettle to boil.

"Your *mamm*, she thinks a mug of hot tea can solve just about everything." His father had been sitting by the giant potbelly stove that warmed the sitting room and kitchen. Now he stood, fed the fire another log and turned to study his son.

"Answered prayers can be difficult things."

"I suppose."

"Have you told her?"

"Told her what?"

"That you care for her."

"Why does it seem that everyone knew how I felt before I did?"

"It was pretty plain to those of us who love you." John sat down and picked up the object he'd been whittling on.

"Is that an alpaca?"

"It is."

"We have the real thing just outside the door."

"Ah, but Rachel doesn't, and she seems to have taken a liking to them."

"So you were preparing for her to leave, before we even saw the news article."

"She was never ours to have." His *dat* peered over the reading glasses he wore whenever he worked on his small wood projects.

Caleb sank onto the couch, his eyes focused on the

blazing fire, his heart somewhere else entirely. "I have no idea what to do."

"If you want good advice, consult an old man."

"Things were different for you, when you were courting *Mamm*. It was a simpler time."

"You think so?"

"Wasn't it?"

"Your mother, her people are over in Ohio…"

"I'm aware."

"I'd gone to work on a mission project in the area, after a tornado had passed through."

Caleb sat up straighter. "You never told me that."

"You never asked."

"How could I have when I didn't know—"

"Your *mamm*, she was, she is the baby of the family. Everyone else had moved off. I didn't think she'd want to leave her parents. She felt…responsible for them, I guess."

"But you asked her."

"I did. I was afraid to, like you're afraid now. I told myself it would be better if she didn't know how I felt, but your *mamm* already knew. She only needed to hear it from me."

"And she agreed to come here—to Indiana."

"*Ya*—eventually she did."

"What of her parents?"

"They moved to Maine, where one of her *bruders* had settled with his family."

"I don't remember any of this."

"They died somewhat young, at least it seems that way to me now. Funny how our idea of old age changes the more years we tack on. But they were happy there. And your *mamm*? I believe she's been happy here."

Caleb could lean forward and just see Rachel and his *mamm* sitting at the table. Both were cradling mugs of tea, the steam rising. Rachel seemed calmer. Perhaps his *mamm* was right. Maybe a mug of hot tea could cure many things—including homesickness and regret.

"I know the proper thing is to take her home, and I think it's best if I don't tell her how I feel. She's been through so much already. It would be wrong for me to add one more thing…"

"So you'd make her decision for her." His *dat* had stopped whittling and was watching him now, waiting.

"You think I should tell her."

"I've already said as much. Rachel's a grown woman, with a *gut* head on her shoulders and a big heart. Trust her, and while you're at it give *Gotte* a little credit, that He didn't lead you down this road for no reason. Believe that He has a purpose and a plan."

The evening passed quickly—what Caleb thought of as their last night together. It wasn't. They still had Sunday, but he couldn't help thinking that he wouldn't see her again, that he'd miss her. They exchanged gifts with Rachel. Her cheeks were flushed, and she continually glanced his way. When she handed him a half-finished sweater, he acted as if he was going to slip it on over his clothes.

"*Nein*. You can't wear it until it's done."

"You mean it's not?" He held it up and studied it with one eye closed. "I thought maybe my arm went here," he said, pointing to a hole.

"Give it back." She attempted to pull it away from him as she laughed and blushed.

"So you're going to finish it?"

"I am."

He rubbed his chin and said, "I suppose you could mail it to me."

Suddenly the levity between them vanished, as they all remembered anew that this was their last weekend together.

His *mamm* jumped up to pull a freshly baked peach pie from the oven. His *dat* pretended he needed to add wood to the blazing fire.

"How about a game of checkers?" Caleb asked gruffly.

"I beat you the last three times."

"Which doesn't mean you'll do so again."

He told himself to treasure the memories they were making, but in his heart he kept hearing the echoes of his father's words.

Rachel's a grown woman, with a gut *head on her shoulders and a big heart.*

Trust her.

Give Gotte *a little credit.*

Believe that He has a purpose and a plan.

His *dat* was spot on, as was usually the case. The question was what he planned to do about it.

Chapter Eleven

Rachel had thought the next day would be difficult. They had a quick breakfast and then bundled up to ride together to church—the second service she'd attended with Caleb and his family. This time was completely different. It seemed the Amish grapevine had been hard at work. Everyone had heard the good news about Rachel. The women hugged her or gave her a pat on the arm. The men nodded and smiled as if their own daughter had been found. It seemed natural at lunch to sit with Beth and Gabriel and baby Simon and Caleb.

"I'm going to miss you all," she admitted.

Gabriel darted a glance at Caleb and then he said, "There won't be anyone here to give Caleb a hard time with Christmas plays or inappropriately blue dresses."

"He told you about that?"

Gabriel laughed when Caleb tried to hit him with a roll. He caught it and stuffed half of it in his mouth.

Beth seemed to understand the feelings Rachel was wrestling with. "You can come back in the spring, for the shearing of the alpacas."

She glanced at Caleb, who looked as if he was holding his breath.

"*Ya.* I'd like that."

He reached for her hand under the table, interlaced his fingers with hers. And for a moment she believed that everything was going to be all right. The day passed in a blur of moments that she vowed to hold on to, memories that she hoped would last her until spring.

The next morning, she was worried that goodbyes would be difficult, but it seemed that Rachel had cried herself dry the evening before. All that was left was a dull ache as she realized how much she would miss Ida and John and even the alpacas.

She promised to write.

Ida blinked back her tears, and John continually cleared his throat. By the time Rachel and Caleb boarded the bus, the snow had begun to fall again.

"The bus driver assured me the weather won't slow us down," Caleb said. "In case you were worried."

"I wasn't."

"At least we have plenty of room."

There were only about ten passengers on the bus, but still they'd chosen to sit next to each other. What good was having your own row to stretch out in? Rachel didn't want extra space. She wanted to be with Caleb. But how could she be with him and still be reunited with her family? And what if...what if he didn't even care for her as she did for him?

Did she love Caleb Wittmer?

Could a person fall in love in such a short time?

But then their time together hadn't been ordinary in any way. From the moment she'd opened her eyes in his home and looked up into his face, she'd felt as if she'd been living a fairy tale that was both terrible and wonderful beyond her wildest dreams.

"Nervous about seeing your family?"

"*Nein.* I'm… The thing is that I'm remembering more."

"That's *gut*, right?"

"It is." As the bus pulled out of Montgomery, she told Caleb about her older brother, how they had all doted on him, since he was the only boy in a home with four young girls.

"I suppose he's married."

"He's not, actually. There was an incident with a girl—she left our Amish community to attend an *Englisch* college. It broke Ethan's heart, and he wasn't ready to try again."

"Sounds as if you care for him."

"Very much. He's a hard worker, and a *gut* man. A real blessing to my parents."

"And your *schweschdern*?"

"Miriam is the oldest." She stared out the window, wondering what all she had missed in the last three weeks. Was that how long it had been? Seemed longer. Seemed like a lifetime. "She's expecting, in the spring, I think."

"You'll be an *aenti*."

Rachel smiled at that thought. She could see her sister now, the way her pregnancy had just started to show. Why was it that her memories that had stayed locked away for so long were now washing over her like waves?

"You'll like Clara and Becca. They're younger, but *gut* girls. Clara is the baby of the family—she's nine. She loves to work outside with the animals, especially the goats. One time…" Rachel realized that Caleb had pulled away from her, was rubbing at the middle of his forehead. "Are you feeling ill?"

"Nein."

"Wishing you hadn't—"

"It's nothing like that." He pulled in a deep breath and then slowly released it. "This is where I want to be, Rachel—with you. When you started talking about your family, I realized I hadn't really thought about meeting them."

"You weren't going to simply leave me at the bus station, were you?"

"Your parents said they'd be there to meet you."

"So we wave goodbye and then you start right back home?"

"Not exactly."

"Do they even have another bus going south later today?"

"I don't know." He reached for her hand, intertwined their fingers. "I simply hadn't thought it through."

"You'll be staying the night, Caleb Wittmer, with my family. You can sleep in Ethan's room. There's an extra bed."

"Are you sure I won't be a burden?"

"There's always room for one more in an Amish home."

"I suppose."

"You can go home tomorrow, and be back in time to have Christmas dinner with your parents."

He nodded as if what she said made sense. Rachel sensed a wariness in his eyes, though. Perhaps he was ready to be rid of her, but then she looked down at her hand clasped in his and knew that wasn't true. So why was Caleb nervous about meeting her family? And what could she do to put his mind at ease?

She never expected to fall asleep, but the next thing she knew she was dreaming about playing in a creek—splashing water and throwing a ball as a large dog swam after it.

"We have a Labrador."

"What?" Caleb had been reading the book on alpacas that he'd borrowed from the library. He snapped it shut and adjusted his back against the window so that he could study her.

"A Labrador. She's white and loves to swim." Rachel shook her head, trying to rid herself of the cobwebs. "I think her name is Biscuit."

"Anything else? Anything about…what happened to you?"

"*Nein.* Nothing." She pulled out her knitting to continue working on Caleb's sweater. But she couldn't focus, couldn't remember if she was supposed to knit or purl. Afraid she would mess it up, she set aside the project and began rooting around in the bag that Ida had sent. She pulled out the thermos and a Tupperware container full of peanut-butter squares. As she was passing the snack to Caleb, she looked out the window and saw a large truck pass.

"I rode in one of those."

"That? An eighteen-wheeler?"

"*Ya.* I—I…" Suddenly her throat was dry and her heart was racing. She tried to focus on her breathing, as the counselor had told her. *Don't force the memories, Rachel. Breath and relax, and eventually you will remember the things you've forgotten.*

"Are you okay?"

Caleb's voice sounded as if it was coming to her down a long tunnel. She pushed the container of sweets into his lap and ducked her head between her knees.

"Uh-oh. Are you going to be sick? Should I ask the driver to pull over?"

She shook her head, realized he couldn't see that and forced herself to sit back up. "*Nein.* I was just a little…*narrisch.*"

"Maybe you need to eat." He handed her a peanut-butter bar and unscrewed the cap on the thermos.

She didn't think eating would help, but the worried look on his face was more than she could bear, so she nibbled at the cookie and took a sip of the coffee, then watched another large truck trundle by.

"I remember climbing up into it."

"The truck?"

"*Ya.* I was walking down…down a road, and it was very dark. There was a lot of traffic, and I didn't know…didn't know what to do." The nausea threatened to overwhelm her again, but she breathed deeply and pushed through the memory. What she was remembering wasn't happening to her now. It couldn't hurt her. "I had ridden in a car before that, but then…they were nearly to their destination and so they let me out."

"On the side of the road?"

"*Nein.* A station—a gas station, I guess. It was late, and I didn't want to admit that I was lost." The fear had been nearly paralyzing. She remembered that clearly. How her legs had been shaking, and she'd hopped from the passenger van, assuring the man and woman that she would be fine. "I didn't know what to do, didn't know where I was, and no other cars came, so I started walking…down the highway."

"That must have been terrifying."

"The trucker pulled over on the side of the road, and at first I thought to run, but it had begun to snow, and I was shivering…"

"Do you remember anything about him?"

"Only that he was an older man, a *grossdaddi*. He had pictures of his *grandkinner* tucked up on the dash. I remember thinking he couldn't be bad because of those pictures."

Caleb placed another peanut-butter bar in her hands. She looked down, surprised to find she'd eaten the first. And the nausea? It seemed to be receding.

"Did you maybe leave your coat in the truck?"

"The bathroom." Rachel shook her head, surprised that she could see the truck and the van and the bathroom so clearly. "I took it off in the gas station's bathroom so I could wash my hands. Even took off my *kapp* and bonnet so I could attempt to rebraid my hair. I left them both there, across the top of the stall door."

"And walked out into the cold."

"Didn't even realize it until I was down the road, and then it seemed too far to go back. I remember thinking that if I just kept walking I'd see something I recognized."

"But you didn't."

"We went through a large city… I remember the maze of freeways."

"Indianapolis."

"And then we crossed some farmland, and I looked out and saw… I must have seen an Amish barn, or something that looked familiar. I remember telling the old guy that he could just let me out there. He didn't want to. He kept asking me if I was sure."

"You were in Montgomery then."

"*Ya.* I think so."

They sat silently, Rachel marveling at all that had happened, how she had ended up on Caleb's road—lost and confused. He must have been thinking the same thing, because he leaned forward and rested his forehead against the back of the seat in front of them.

"What are you thinking?" she asked.

"Something that has occurred to me before—that if I hadn't been fixing that portion of fence at the exact moment you stumbled by, that you might have died that night."

"But you were, Caleb." She waited until he glanced over at her. "I don't know what happened, why I was wandering around lost, but I do know—beyond a shadow of a doubt—that *Gotte* was watching out for me, and that His plan for me? It was you."

His plan for me? It was you.

Rachel's words echoed through Caleb's mind as they continued their ride northeast. She knitted as they navigated the freeways of Indianapolis, and then she asked to trade seats as they entered the farming country of northern Indiana. Her nose pressed to the window, she looked like a small child, watching for home.

But Caleb knew she was watching for more clues to her past.

When they entered Nappanee, she began pointing out things to him—Amish Acres and Burkholder Country Store and the Dutch Village Market. The town looked like something out of a postcard, with a light dusting of snow covering the cars and people scurrying about tending to their final Christmas errands—Amish and

Englisch alike, both preparing to celebrate the birth of Christ.

Something inside of Caleb relaxed in that moment. Something changed.

Watching an *Englisch* family pass an Amish one on the sidewalk, he realized that the differences were quite superficial—the way they dressed, the *Englisch* man pausing in front of a car while the Amish man continued two spaces down to a horse and buggy. Both were men spending a few hours in town with their families on a cold Christmas Eve day.

Who was he to say that the Amish folks were better than *Englisch*?

Or that conservative Amish was better than those communities that were a tad more progressive? He noticed the woman was wearing a bright blue dress, nearly the color of the one Rachel had been wearing that first day, the color he had found so inappropriate. Why had that mattered to him so much? Now that he knew Rachel, and he did believe that he knew her well, he understood that she was a *gut* woman. But he might have missed knowing that, or anything else about her, simply because he dismissed her out of hand over the color of the fabric of her dress.

Perhaps he had spent too much of his life determined to emphasize the differences between his community and others.

He'd done it for good reasons.

Fear that the Amish lifestyle might fade away.

Worry that if he had a family, it wouldn't be possible to raise children as he'd been raised.

Anxiety that their faith might become less important, and their ambition more so.

The answer to those concerns was prayer, not stubbornness. He could see that now as clearly as he could see the color that had blossomed in Rachel's cheeks. *Gotte* had prepared a path for her, and that path had included Caleb.

If his Heavenly Father could be trusted with this dear woman sitting beside him, with her care and welfare even at her most vulnerable moment, then Caleb could trust that He was looking out for their faith and community, as well.

"Why are you looking at me that way?" Rachel placed her hand on the top of her head. "My *kapp* falling off?"

"Nein."

"Color of my dress is okay, right?"

"Now you're giving me a hard time."

"I want to make sure I'm presentable." Her smile practically sparkled. "Am I?"

Caleb's heart filled with gratitude. He didn't know what their future held, but he did know that Rachel was going to be okay. "What did you ask me?"

"If I look presentable. If my dress is okay." She bumped her shoulder against his.

"It's fine—quite pretty."

"Why, thank you, Caleb Wittmer."

"You're welcome, Rachel Yoder."

Then they were pulling into the Goshen bus stop, where only one family stood waiting—one family, but three buggies. He could tell they were together because they were huddled in a group—men, women and *youngies*. It would seem that the entire family had come to welcome Rachel home.

The next few hours passed in a blur.

Caleb was introduced to Deborah and Clarence, Rachel's parents. Clarence was a tall man, tall and thin. He pumped Caleb's hand, thanking him repeatedly for bringing Rachel home. Deborah looked like an older version of Rachel, right down to the freckles. She pulled him into a hug and whispered, "*Gotte* bless you, Caleb. *Gotte* bless you for your kindness."

He said hello to Clara and Becca, but they looked so much alike that he couldn't remember who was who. Miriam was easy enough to pick out because of the fact that she was in at least her second trimester of pregnancy. Her husband, Clyde, stood holding his wife's hand and beaming at Rachel. It was obvious they had all been very worried, and now on Christmas Eve of all days, that worry had been taken away.

Ethan nodded toward the newest buggy and said, "Care to ride with me? I have to stop by a friend's and pick up one last Christmas gift. Unless you're too tired…"

"*Nein.* That sounds *gut.*" He suspected that as the eldest child Ethan had some questions for him, but instead he started their conversation by explaining what had occurred on their end.

Ethan told him how they'd first thought Rachel had simply left for the weekend, and then everyone became increasingly more worried when she didn't call or write.

"But we knew she carried that book of poetry everywhere, so I thought…"

"You're the one who wrote the article in *The Budget.*"

Ethan was a few years older than Caleb. He scratched at his clean-shaven jaw and shrugged. "I wrote something like it, gave it to our scribe. She cleaned it up and submitted it to the paper."

"Your parents never called the police?"

"*Nein.* They talked to them, but our local sheriff has been here a long time. He's aware that Amish *youngies* sometimes leave town with no word—there's less conflict that way."

"Does that happen a lot?" Caleb's old worries of the Amish way of life disintegrating popped back into his mind, but he refused to dwell on them. *Youngies* came and went. It was true in every community. He'd heard it was true among the *Englisch*, as well. It was a time of transition, and when faced with such a decision, some chose a different path.

"Not a lot, but some. Enough that our sheriff wouldn't take the case seriously until we had something else to suggest there had been foul play."

"When I found Rachel, she didn't remember anything—not her name or where she was from. She still struggles with some of the effects of the amnesia. Her memories—they're not all back yet."

"And your family took her in."

"If your *mamm* is anything like mine, you know that wasn't even a question. Of course we took her in."

Ethan pulled off his hat and resettled it on his head. The buggy was tolerably warm with a small heater in the front, and snow continued to fall lightly. But Ethan's mind obviously wasn't on the weather or even where he was going. Caleb could practically see him trying to piece together the time line of what had happened.

"You found her? In the snow? Was she hurt at all? Did she really not know where she was?"

Caleb couldn't blame him for questioning his story. What had that been like, to have your sister simply vanish?

"Yes, yes, not at all and no—she didn't even know her name, let alone where she was."

Ethan grunted, "It's what *Mamm* told us, what Rachel told her. Just so hard to believe."

"Trust me. It's something I won't forget no matter if I live to be a very old man—the sight of her weaving down the road, wearing no coat or *kapp* and then collapsing in the snow."

"You took her to the doctor?"

"We have a small hospital, really more of a medical clinic. The doctors there looked her over, made sure she wasn't hurt in any way."

"Other than losing her memory and nearly freezing."

"She also had a bump on the back of her head."

"What?"

"Maybe she forgot to mention that to your *mamm*. She had a big bump on the back of her head. She still doesn't remember how it happened, but that's what caused her memory loss."

"How did she end up so far from here?"

"She remembered a little of that on the way here." Caleb told him what Rachel had shared with him on the bus.

"You've been a *gut* friend to her."

Caleb almost corrected him, almost confessed his feelings for Rachel there and then, but they were pulling into an Amish home with a small sign out front that read Rugs For Sale. When they'd picked up the Christmas present Ethan had ordered, they turned back toward the Yoder home, stopping at the local grocer to buy three gallons of ice cream.

"I'd almost forgotten it's Christmas Eve," Caleb admitted.

"*Ya*. It is, but this…" Ethan patted the grocery bag on the seat. "This is a homecoming present. Rachel might not remember, but peppermint is her favorite ice cream."

They rode in silence the rest of the way home.

The house they pulled up to was much larger than the one Caleb had been raised in, but then the Yoders had five children, plus Miriam's husband and soon their child. Plainly, they were prepared for the family to keep expanding.

Ethan pulled the horse and buggy into the barn.

It was while they were removing the harness and stabling the horse that Caleb thought to ask Ethan something. "Did she have a beau?"

"Rachel?"

"*Ya*." It occurred to him that there had been only family members waiting for them at the bus drop-off.

"*Nein*. Rachel was trying to find her way. She was struggling a bit. That's why, at first, we thought she'd simply needed some time to clear her head."

"Would that have been like her? To just…walk away? To tell no one?" It certainly didn't sound like the Rachel that he knew. But then, maybe she'd been a different person before.

"It wasn't like her at all. Look…" Ethan paused at the door to the barn before pushing out into the gathering dusk. "The week before? It had been hard on Rachel. I don't know how much she remembers, or if she'd even want me sharing the details with you, but we are grateful that she's home, that you and your family cared for her."

And then they were walking toward the house on a snowy Christmas Eve, Caleb shouldering more questions than ever.

* * *

Rachel's heart was so full of emotion that she felt like a balloon that had been overfilled and was about to burst.

That described exactly how she felt.

About to burst with happiness.

Her younger sisters sat on each side of her, as if they were afraid she might disappear again. Miriam kept smiling at her, one hand placed on her stomach, the other holding Clyde's hand. Her mother sat by her father, as he prepared to read the Christmas story. Ethan and Caleb rounded out their group. Each time she glanced around the room, one of them was watching her.

A conversation that she'd had with Ethan came back to her then. It had been the night before her accident, or whatever she'd had. They'd been in the barn together, and she'd been aggravated with everyone—her parents, her older sister, even the younger girls. They'd all grated on her nerves and she'd felt so suffocated, so out of place, that she'd said something to Ethan about it. His response had surprised her.

"Home is where you belong. It may not be where you always stay, but it's the place that fits—like an old shoe. It's why we keep returning to it over and again, no matter how old we become or how far away we move."

His words had only served to frustrate her more. He'd said them as if things were so clear, so simple, and she didn't think they were. He'd been right, though. She knew that now, knew it with a certainty that she couldn't have imagined then.

She cleared her throat and sat up straighter. "I know *Dat*'s about to read the story of the Baby Jesus. I know that's our tradition—what we've always done. I remember that much, even though a few days ago I didn't know my own last name."

Light laughter filtered through the group.

"We're glad you're here now."

"*Gotte* is *gut*."

"We thought you simply wanted to get out of chores for a few days."

She waited until they'd quieted down again, until she had their attention, because this was important, and she thought she could only get through it once.

"I still don't remember everything, don't remember how I lost my memory, though I remember being lost."

Now there were murmurs of sympathy and Becca on her right and Clara on her left reached for her hands.

"I do remember the night before." She waited for Ethan to look up, to nod slightly. "I was feeling out of sorts, as if everyone had a purpose in their life and understood what it was—everyone except me."

She stopped, her throat clogged with the tears she didn't want to shed.

Her *mamm* leaned forward and waited for her to meet her gaze. "We've all felt that way at times, dear."

"I understand that now, that what I was feeling was probably normal. At the time, I didn't, though. I went outside, hoping to clear my head, and made my way to the barn."

"Where you found me," Ethan said.

"And I asked you—I can remember this as clearly as if it were this afternoon—I asked you…"

"What if I never find where I belong." They said the words together and their eyes locked, as an understanding of that night and all that had transpired since passed between them.

Rachel glanced at Caleb, who was sitting forward now, listening intently.

"Ethan said, 'Home is where you belong.'" She swiped at the tears slipping down her face. "He said it as if it was a simple fact, like it's going to snow tomorrow or daylight will arrive at six thirty. He said it as if there was no doubt. But me? I had plenty of doubts."

Her *dat* stared down at the open Bible in his lap. When he looked up, a gentle smile eased the worry lines around his eyes. "We're so glad you're home, so grateful to Caleb and his family, and mostly thankful to *Gotte* that He watched over you."

"I know that now, *Dat*. I know that home, that here with you all, is exactly where I belong." She wanted to add "until *Gotte* has other plans," but suddenly everyone was talking at once, everyone except for Caleb, who was watching her as if she'd just said the one thing that could break his heart.

Chapter Twelve

❧

Rachel woke Christmas morning to the smells that she'd known all her life—a fire in the stove downstairs, cedar sprigs placed throughout the house, cinnamon rolls in the oven, coffee percolating on the stove. She made her way downstairs and found her *mamm* sitting at the table.

"Gudemariye, Mamm."

"And to you, Rachel." She waited until Rachel had poured a mug of coffee and sat down across from her. "I want to explain to you why we didn't call the police…"

"You don't have to do that."

"I do, for me." She traced the rim of her mug with her thumb. "I was terrified, when you didn't come home that first night. I hope you never know that sort of fear, wondering where your child had gone, wondering what you could have done differently."

"I'm sorry that I put you through that."

"You remember nothing of the fight we had?"

"Nein." The word was a whisper, nothing more than a breath carried over an aching heart.

"You wanted to quit your job, your apprenticeship at the school."

"I was teaching?"

Her mother studied her a moment and finally nodded. "You had tried several jobs, but none of them suited you. Oh, they were fine jobs, as far as jobs go, but you weren't satisfied."

"I wanted more."

"You kept saying that it wasn't what you were meant to do, as if you had some destiny beyond being a *gut* wife and mother. I didn't understand that. Just as I didn't understand why you broke up with Samuel."

Rachel covered her mouth with her hand. "Samuel King. He was two years younger than me, and I thought...I thought he was a child."

Her *mamm* leaned forward, pulled Rachel's hands across the table and covered them with her own. "Sweetheart, I've had a lot of time to think since you've been gone, a lot of time to pray. I want to say I'm so sorry..."

"This wasn't your fault."

"I'm so sorry that I didn't attempt to understand what you were going through more."

"How could you?"

Her *mamm* stared into her eyes a moment, as if she was searching for something. Finally, she patted Rachel's hand, sat back and took another sip from her coffee. "Our life is simple—Plain. Our choices are few, and we like it that way. Only three dresses to choose from, only a few jobs, only a handful of beaus."

"I don't think a dozen beaus or job choices would have satisfied me at that point. I was...lost."

"And that's okay. *Gotte* had a plan for you, whether

we understood it or not. I'm just so grateful you're home."

Rachel didn't think her heart could hurt any more than it already did, but seeing her mother cry opened a whole new chasm inside of her. She hopped up, stumbled around the table and threw herself into her mother's arms.

That was how her *dat* and Ethan and Caleb found them as they stamped their feet in the mudroom and then plodded into the kitchen with Christmas greetings on their lips. Deborah and Rachel jumped up and began pulling together things for the family breakfast. It was traditional to keep it rather simple—some sweet rolls, milk for the youngsters, coffee for those who were older.

They'd have a family devotional, spend time considering the miracle of Christ's birth, and then later they'd have a big lunch with extended family. In the evening they would exchange gifts. But as her large family tumbled into the room and around the table, Rachel realized that the most precious moment of the holiday was occurring right then. She'd been reunited with her family. The rift that had existed between her and her mother—a rift that she hadn't been able to remember but knew in her heart was there—had been healed. The only thing to mar the near perfect morning was the fact that Caleb would be leaving before lunch, and she didn't know if she'd ever see him again.

Caleb rode in the back seat of the buggy, with Rachel on his left and both of her younger sisters on his right. Ethan was driving the buggy, and Miriam's husband, Clyde, was sitting next to him in the front seat. The entire family had wanted to see him off, but they'd decided to limit it to one buggy.

Caleb had wanted a moment alone with Rachel. He had to satisfy himself with being jostled against her as Clara and Becca prattled on about seeing their cousins, and how much snow they'd had, and presents that would be opened later that evening.

He'd about given up on the hope of speaking privately with Rachel, when they pulled up to the bus stop and Ethan said, "Rachel, we'll wait here if you'd like to walk with Caleb to get his ticket."

The girls fell into a chorus of "not fair" and "we want to go," but Clyde distracted them with a game of I Spy.

Rachel and Caleb walked to the store where tickets were usually sold, but taped on the window was a sign that read:

Closed for Christmas. If you're waiting for a bus, purchase your ticket from the driver.

"You don't have to wait," Caleb said.

"I want to."

"I bought you a Christmas present."

"You already gave me one."

"A skein of yarn? That wasn't your real gift."

"I love yarn."

"I have another for you, but I left it at home." Why had he done that? He'd known this would be goodbye.

"Your sweater...it's not finished yet."

"A fine pair we are." He reached for her hand, instantly feeling better when their fingers were laced together.

They huddled under the overhang of the building's roof, waiting on the bus that should arrive in the next ten minutes. Ten minutes. How was he supposed to tell her what was on his heart in so short a time? But then his watch ticked off another two minutes, and he knew that he had to try.

Rachel was talking about her family, apologizing for the chaos and her sisters and the fact that they weren't as traditional as he was used to.

"I don't care about any of that."

"Excuse me?"

"I need to tell you something, Rachel."

"You do?"

"But I don't want… I don't want you to answer me, not now." He reached out, tucked a wayward lock of hair into her *kapp* and allowed his fingers to linger on her cheek.

"I'm so fortunate that you found me."

"*Nein.* I'm the fortunate one. I love you, Rachel Yoder."

"You do?"

"I know our lives are very different."

"Not so different."

"And I live a long way from here."

"Only five hours."

"I know that you need time with your family, time to be home."

"I do?"

"You need time to remember, time to understand who you are and what you want in life."

"I want you." She seemed as surprised as he was at that confession.

Three of the sweetest words Caleb had ever heard, but he knew with complete certainty that now wasn't their time to make any big decisions. He heard the bus pulling into the parking area. Leaning closer, he kissed her once and then again. He pressed his forehead to hers, and then he said, "I'll write."

"You will?"

"And call."

"I'm going to miss you."

"I love you," he said again, aware that she hadn't said those words yet, that she wasn't ready yet. It confirmed that he was doing the right thing leaving her there, leaving her with her family. He kissed her once more, then pushed his hat down on his head and jogged toward the bus.

Rachel watched Caleb jog away and she wanted to sit down, put her head on her arms and weep. When her life was finally coming together, when things were finally starting to make sense, why did he have to leave?

Had he really said he loved her?

She walked back to the buggy in a daze.

Her little sisters had moved on from I Spy to playing finger games with pieces of yarn they both kept in their pockets. Clyde was looking out the window and saying that by this time next year he would be a father. But Ethan's gaze met hers, and she knew he knew.

Had Caleb spoken to him?

Or did she simply have a love-dazed look about her? Because she was in love with Caleb Wittmer. For the life of her, she couldn't think of why she hadn't told him, but she would. In time, she would.

The day passed in a flurry of family and celebration and gift giving. Though their holidays were dramatically scaled back as compared to *Englischers'* celebration, the fact that they had over twenty people in the house with her *aentis* and *onkels* and grandparents and cousins meant that there wasn't a quiet moment. And though she felt terrible that she had no gifts for anyone—she hadn't known she'd be back home and, in fact, she still had Caleb's sweater in her bag waiting to be finished—that didn't stop everyone from stacking gifts around her.

She received a new coat, gloves, mittens, an outdoor bonnet, a scarf and a small book of poetry. Her *mamm* gave her a basket overflowing with writing supplies— stationery, a new pen, envelopes and stamps. She kissed Rachel's cheek and whispered, "Maybe you can write to Caleb," which was what she thought about doing for the next hour. But she fell into bed without uncapping the pen, a whirlwind of emotions clouding her thoughts. She was exhausted, heartsick that Caleb was gone and tremendously happy to finally be home.

New Year's Day arrived with a blizzard that kept everyone inside. Rachel finally began writing Caleb. She had tried several times before that. Each night she'd sat in front of her little desk, pulled the paper toward her and stared at it.

What could she say to him that he didn't already know about her?

How could she describe her feelings?

When could she expect to see him again?

The questions swirled and collided in her mind until she would invariably push the paper away, climb into bed and huddle under the covers. She was still grateful to be home, but a malaise had settled over her feelings until it felt as if she was viewing everything from a distance. She constantly berated herself for feeling blue. She should feel grateful! Had she learned nothing from her time away from home? Yet no matter how much she told herself that she should feel happy, she often found herself on the verge of tears.

After she cleared the breakfast dishes, her *mamm* suggested she spend some time on the sun porch.

"It's still snowing."

"Not on the porch."

"I'll freeze."

"We put windows in years ago and a small butane heater. Remember?"

Rachel nodded, but in truth she didn't remember at all. There was much she still couldn't recall, though each day brought at least one new revelation about her past—she couldn't abide peas, she was the family's designated baker, she visited the local library at least once a week, she had a kitten named Stripes that slept in the office in the barn.

"There's a rocker and even a small desk there," her *mamm* continued. Rachel's younger sisters were playing jacks in the barn, Miriam had gone to her mother-in-law's for the week and Ethan and her *dat* were in the barn working on a table that they planned to sell at the next auction. Only Rachel and her *mamm* remained in the house. It was quiet and forced Rachel's thoughts to address questions she didn't have answers to. The entire thing made her want to go back upstairs, back to bed.

"You know, your *dat* built the porch for me because I sometimes suffer from winter blues, or seasonal depression, as the *Englisch* doctor calls it."

"I thought he built the porch for us kids."

"It was a *wunderbaar* place for you all to get a bit of sunshine when the weather kept us in for days on end, but *nein*, he built it for me."

"And did it help?"

"*Ya.* As a matter of fact it did."

"Do you think I'm depressed, *Mamm*?"

"I don't know. What do you think?"

"Maybe."

"How's your energy level?"

"Low to nonexistent. It's as if I have the flu, but I don't."

"Moody?"

"You know I am. You caught me crying when I spilled the flour on the floor yesterday."

"Problems sleeping?"

"I toss and turn a lot."

"Perhaps we should make an appointment with the doctor."

Rachel shrugged. "I'm still a little confused, a little lost, and I miss Caleb." She hesitated, not sure if she was ready to share her deepest fears yet.

Instead of pushing her to say more, her *mamm* went to the kitchen, brewed two mugs of hot tea and brought them back. That kindness reminded her of Ida and gave her the courage to speak her fears. "What if Caleb doesn't really care about me?"

"So you think he doesn't know his own mind?"

"What if those feelings arose out of the oddness of our situation? He saved a coatless girl who might have died in the snow. Maybe that's not love he feels. Maybe it's relief or surprise or merely affection."

"Have you written him yet? Have you asked Caleb these things?"

"*Nein.* I want to. I mean to, but then when I sit down…I don't know what to say."

"Say what's in your heart, dear."

So with her *mamm* claiming that it would be a lovely place to write a letter, Rachel found herself alone on the sun porch. The new pen and paper waited before her as snow billowed outside the window. She noticed the calendar on the wall, stood up and pulled it off the hook.

Scanning back through the months, she marveled at all that had happened. If she had known what she would endure, she might have hidden upstairs the entire year. But those trials had brought her Caleb, and she would never wish away the times they had shared. She carried the old calendar to the desk, opened the drawer and pulled out the new one that her father always picked up at the hardware store. Opening it, she saw a beautiful sunrise over fields laden with snow. Across the bottom was printed:

Hope smiles from the threshold of the year to come,
Whispering, "It will be happier."
Alfred Lord Tennyson

Did she believe that? Could she trust *Gotte* that this New Year would be happier, would be better than the last?

She stared out the window, glanced back at the calendar. She prayed, she doodled and finally the words began to flow.

January 1
Dear Caleb,
You must think terribly of me, since I've yet to write. I received your postcard and your letter. Thank you so much. I've wanted to write to you, but when I try, my thoughts and feelings become tangled. Do you think that what we feel for each other could be situational? Do you worry that

when I regain all of my memories, and life finally returns to normal, when spring comes and you are busy with your alpacas and farming…do you think we will feel the same?

Please give my best to your parents.
Sincerely,
Rachel

She sealed the envelope, carried it out to the mailbox and tried to fill the rest of the day with useful activities. The hours seemed hollow, though. She felt as if she was walking in a dream that she couldn't quite wake from.

Caleb's reply arrived so quickly that she marveled at the efficiency of the postal service. Her mother handed her the letter and nodded toward the sunroom. She settled at the desk and tore it open with shaking hands.

January 6
Dear Rachel,
I check the mailbox each day, sure that I will find a letter from you, and today that dream came true.

I am pleased to hear that you do have feelings for me, and I am sure that the love I feel for you is genuine and lasting. It may have begun when I picked you up out of the snow, but remember I didn't even like you very much then. I hope that line made you laugh or at least smile.

The alpacas don't seem to mind the snow. Their coats have become quite thick. I'm looking forward to the first shearing.
My regards to your family and my deepest feelings for you,
Caleb

A week later, she received a nice fat envelope from Montgomery, Indiana. In it was a circle letter from Ida to Deborah. Ida spoke of her crochet work, updated Rachel on the families she'd met in the area and asked what types of flowers they planted in the spring. John wrote a half a page below that, the comments directed more to Rachel's father, although one line assured Rachel that they continued to pray for her each day.

And below both of those messages were two pages from Caleb. He spoke to Ethan about the alpacas. Rachel hadn't realized Ethan was interested in the animals. Her *mamm* paused in reading the letter as Rachel told them how she'd named each one, and how they acted when they were spooked, and how gentle they could be if you fed them carrots.

"Can we get one?" Becca asked.

"We'll help. We promise we will," Clara chimed in.

At the bottom of Caleb's writing, he wrote a personal line to each person in the family. The letter surprised Rachel. Though his tone was informal, it reminded her of the letters her friends had received, years ago when she was first out of school. They would hear of a boy in another community, or perhaps the boy had visited a relative in their area, and the boy would begin to write—not merely to the girl, but to the family. It was a sort of long-distance courting, this getting to know one another.

Was Caleb courting her?

Is that what his letter meant?

Her *mamm* was holding up another envelope, but Rachel had missed whatever she'd said.

"What?"

"There's another letter here."

"It's for me?"

"Seems to be. It's a smaller envelope that was inside this large one, and your name is on the outside."

Her younger sisters began making kissing sounds, Ethan asked to see the portion about the alpacas and her father picked up *The Budget* after winking at her.

As if she was in a dream, Rachel stood, walked across the room and accepted the small envelope. Her fingers traced her name on the outside. She glanced up at her *mamm.*

"Perhaps you'd like to read it in the sunroom."

"*Ya.* I would."

Which caused Clara and Becca to fall into a fit of giggles.

Rachel paid them no mind. Caleb had written to her before. She'd lived with his family for nearly a month. Why did this seem different? Why was her heart hammering and her pulse racing?

She hurried to the sunroom and sat in the rocker, near the small heater, which she cranked to high.

The room was cheery even on a dark winter evening. Her *mamm* had used yellow and green and blue fabric to sew several lap throws that were scattered around the room. An afghan made from variegated purple yarn was folded and placed in a basket near her feet. She pulled the afghan across her lap and opened the envelope.

Dearest Rachel,
I hope you enjoyed my letter to your family. I suppose it might appear quite old-fashioned, to write to a girl's family, but as you know I'm an old-fashioned sort of guy. Your letter caused me to realize that perhaps I haven't made my intentions clear. Oh, I blurted out my feelings casu-

ally enough, no doubt flabbergasting you as you stood under the overhang of the store on a snowy Christmas morning. I meant what I said then, and I'll say it again here—I love you, Rachel Yoder, and I'd like to court you. I realize long-distance relationships are difficult, and I know that you are still recovering from your accident. I'd like to hear more about the things you are remembering, the things you worry about and how well you are settling in. I want to know everything about you, Rachel.

It occurs to me that we barely know one another, and yet I remain affectionately yours,
Caleb

She read the letter twice more, and then she moved to the table in the corner of the room, pulled her stationery toward her and began to write. She poured out her heart in a way that she hadn't in the first letter. She found herself filling page after page, telling him about her mother's seasonal depression, that she might suffer from the same, and describing the sunroom to him. She held nothing back, and why would she? If he cared about her, then he wouldn't run from such revelations. And if he did run, then he wasn't the man she thought he was.

Chapter Thirteen

Caleb had never thought of himself as an impatient man, but waiting for spring, waiting for an opportunity to go and visit Rachel—that took all the patience he could muster. They continued exchanging letters through January and February, and finally, in March, the last of the snow melted.

"Give her our love," his *mamm* said, pushing a lunch sack into his hands as the bus pulled into the parking area.

"And tell her *dat* that I hope to meet him someday." Caleb's father winked. They'd talked about his relationship with Rachel on several occasions. He knew how Caleb felt, and he was the one who had suggested that Caleb write to the whole family. "Show her you want to be a part of her entire life, not just make her a part of yours."

The ride to Goshen was more familiar this time. He passed through Indianapolis without gawking at the skyscrapers, and he breathed a sigh of relief when they navigated the highway interchange and popped out the other side. Caleb knew he was getting close once he saw the signs for Nappanee.

The plan was to stay for a week, attend the auction in Shipshewana and speak to both Rachel's parents and her bishop about his intentions—if she still felt the same way. Their letters had been filled with everyday tidbits, but they rarely wrote about their feelings. He didn't want to push her. He certainly didn't want to rush her, and he could tell from her letters that the time at home was doing exactly what it should—it was healing both her heart and her mind.

Ethan and Rachel were waiting for him when the bus pulled into Goshen. He gazed out at the blustery spring day, at the woman that he had thought of and dreamed of and prayed for, and he felt as if his heart was taking flight like a child's kite.

Rachel waited at the buggy, one hand patting the buggy horse as the other held her *kapp* on her head. Ethan jogged up to see if he needed help with his bags.

Caleb stood staring at her, his suitcase in one hand, his hat in the other, until Ethan slapped him on the back and said, "She's doing better—our Rachel is."

And those two words—*our Rachel*—helped him to start moving toward her again.

Her color was better, the dark circles under her eyes were gone and a ready smile played on her lips. She'd gained some needed weight. She looked more like a woman and less like a lost girl. Her dress was a pale green, freshly laundered and covered with a white apron.

She looked more beautiful than he remembered.

He wasn't sure how to greet her.

Ethan must have sensed their awkwardness because

he muttered, "I think there's something I was supposed to pick up in the store," and gave them a few minutes alone.

Rachel cocked her head, her smile widened and she looked directly into his eyes. "How are you, Caleb?"

"*Gut*, and you…you look fabulous."

And then his heart won over any thoughts of impropriety.

He dropped his bag on the ground, crammed his hat on his head and closed the gap between them. Rachel stepped into his arms, and he was content for the first time since Christmas Day.

On the ride to the Yoder farm, Ethan continued to pepper him with questions about the alpacas. He planned to go with Caleb to the auction, and he hoped to purchase a few of his own. He asked about shearing and mating and feeding and bedding.

Caleb tried to answer intelligently, but his mind was on the woman in the front seat of the buggy.

If he'd thought they'd have time alone when he reached the house, he was mistaken. Rachel's little sisters were home, and they insisted he follow them to the barn, peek in on the new foal and pet the newest litter of kittens. He thought the time spent with Ethan and Clarence would be pure torture, but he finally relaxed, realized Rachel wasn't going anywhere and enjoyed the time with her *bruder* and *dat*. After all, her family would be his family if this trip was the success he'd prayed for.

Dinner was a busy, raucous affair, especially with Miriam's new infant, a boy that they had named Stephen.

"We all call him baby Stevie," Clara explained. "Stephen sounds old, and he's not going to be old for years and years yet."

"He won't let you call him that when he goes to school," Becca reminded her.

"That won't be for a long time."

"Time flies."

"I wish this dinnertime would fly so I wouldn't have to listen to you."

"That's enough, girls." Deborah gave her youngest daughters a serious look. They waited until she'd turned her back to make faces at each other.

Later that evening, Rachel asked him, "Is my family too much?"

"What do you mean?"

"Too loud, boisterous, nosy… I almost died when Becca asked if you'd kissed me yet."

They were sitting in two rockers in the sunroom he'd barely noticed during his first visit—the sunroom that Rachel had told him so much about.

"I want to kiss you again right now."

"You do?"

"*Ya*, but I believe your parents can see us from the sitting room."

"I'm sure they can."

So he reached over and snagged her hand instead, laced his fingers with hers and said, "Tell me about this porch. What you've done, it's amazing."

"I told you about my *mamm*'s seasonal depression. She says she doesn't suffer from it as much as she once did, and the doctor we visited, he said it's related to our hormones and that's why hers is better."

"So you only have, what…twenty or thirty more years to deal with it."

She laughed when he said that, and another part of Caleb relaxed.

"The doctor offered medicine, which I will take if I need to, but so far things are better, and I guess…I guess it's because I've finally found what I feel satisfied doing."

"This room has Rachel written all over it."

"*Mamm* said to think of it as my room, my shop."

A display of finished knitted projects adorned an open cabinet with small handwritten prices affixed to each item. Another part of the room was dedicated to turning the lamb's wool she'd purchased into yarn. It included a basket with several sizes of carding paddles. There were also spools and cardboard spindles, a spinning wheel and what looked like several jars of dye.

"How did you learn to do all of this?"

"There's an older woman in our church who taught me some of it. The rest, I checked out books from the library and searched for information on the computer."

They both laughed at the mention of a library computer, remembering that long-ago argument about what was and wasn't proper.

Colorful skeins of yarn hung from hooks along one wall. Rachel stood and pulled him over to them. "These are the color of the sheep's wool, and these I dyed myself."

"What did you use?"

"All natural things because people who purchase the yarn or the finished items, many of them are *Englischers*, and they want to know that no harsh chemicals are used."

"What sort of natural things?"

"Berries mostly, evergreen for those and roots for the browns."

She showed him some of her finished things—sweaters and blankets and scarves and baby blankets.

"It's hard to believe that you've done all this since Christmas."

"I've had a lot of time on my hands, and *Mamm* was right when she says it's best to keep busy."

"You sound better. You have sounded better for many weeks now."

Rachel nodded, her *kapp* strings bouncing, and he was reminded of her lying in the snow, her hair fanned out around her and her complexion frighteningly pale.

Pulling him back over to the rocking chairs, she lowered her voice—not so her family wouldn't hear. They had to already know what she was telling him, but perhaps it was simply difficult for her to discuss.

"At first, I thought my depression was a result of the accident."

"You wrote that your doctor said that was possible."

"It's so embarrassing, to admit to having these feelings…"

"Please don't be embarrassed with me. I care about you."

She squeezed his hand, then leaned back and set her rocker into motion. "I'm learning that many people care about me. Only, I couldn't see that before. Apparently, this has been a problem since I first left school, and my parents wanted me to speak to the bishop or see a doctor, but I refused."

"Because you were ashamed?"

"I suppose, or maybe I thought it wouldn't do any good."

Caleb rubbed his thumb over the grain of the rocking chair's arm. No doubt Ethan had made the chair. He was a fine carpenter.

"When my *mamm* finally told me how she suffered with the same thing, I didn't feel like such a freak anymore."

"You're not a freak. You're a beautiful, kind woman."

"Some of it is seasonal, we think. It's called SAD—seasonal affective disorder."

"And you said that you're not taking any medicine for it."

"Not at this time—perhaps I will next winter, if I need it. But this room...the sunshine helps. Doing something I love."

"The knitting."

"*Ya*, it helps, too."

Which left Caleb with quite the predicament, because he wanted to ask Rachel to marry him. He had come here to do that very thing, but how could he take her from a place where she was flourishing? How could he ask her to move away from the family that cared so much for her?

Yet he couldn't move away from his parents.

He was their only child.

He simply could not leave them alone.

"Do you have a headache?" Rachel jumped up. "*Mamm* has some over-the-counter medicine."

"It's okay. I'm just tired, I think."

It was later that evening, when he was tossing and turning in the extra bed in Ethan's room, that Rachel's brother finally said, "Maybe if you talk about it, you'll stop keeping me awake."

So they did, and that turned out to be a very good thing.

Because suddenly, without any doubt, Caleb knew exactly what he needed to do.

Rachel barely had any time alone with Caleb.

On Friday they visited the auction. Ethan purchased a half dozen alpacas. Caleb and Ethan went back on Saturday to see to their delivery.

Sunday dawned sunny and beautiful.

Though they could still often have winter weather in March in northern Indiana, for the day at least, spring had arrived.

Rachel put on her Sunday dress, fussed over her hair, which she then covered with a *kapp*, and made her way downstairs.

"Caleb is out in the barn with Ethan and your *dat*."

"I thought he might be."

"He's a nice young man, Rachel. I think *Gotte* brought you two together at the exact time when you needed each other most."

Rachel didn't answer that because she didn't know how.

She had thought for a moment the night before that Caleb was going to ask her to marry him—but then his mood had suddenly changed, and he'd gone to bed. Was he having second thoughts? She'd been completely honest with him about her moods, about her condition, and she wouldn't blame him if he decided that she was too much to take on. At the same time, she was no longer ashamed of her condition, or of the feelings she struggled with.

She understood that everyone she met was dealing

with something. It was only that some people's struggles were more visible than others.

Rachel felt good now, stronger, but she knew there would still be dark days ahead.

Now that she knew why, that thought didn't frighten her as much as it once had.

The Sunday service was one of the finest that she remembered—the preaching was particularly moving, the singing beautiful and the luncheon delicious. Caleb spent some of the time with her, but he also went off with her *bruder* to join a game of baseball, and once she saw him speaking with their bishop. It was a *wunderbaar* day, but she'd barely spent any time alone with him. The next week would fly by, and then he'd be returning home.

What had she expected to happen?

Her life wasn't a romance novel, where the beau dropped to one knee and pulled out a sparkling diamond ring. They didn't even wear rings. And yet, a part of her had thought that something would be settled between them.

They had nothing scheduled for Monday, and her *bruder* and *dat* had committed to helping a neighbor repair his barn. Caleb offered to go with them, but Ethan shook his head, her *dat* said, "Not necessary, but *danki*," and her *mamm* pushed another cup of coffee into his hands.

"Perhaps Rachel could take you to see the schoolhouse, where she used to teach. It's a pleasant walk."

Caleb had grown up attending a one-room schoolhouse, same as she had, same as nearly every Amish child did. She didn't think there would be much for him to see there, but then again they had nothing else planned. The day had turned slightly cooler and rain was expected before the end of the week. Clouds scudded across the sky, occasionally blocking the sun.

She supposed her life was like the sky. Some days would be sunny and others filled with rain. The thought caused her to think of blue, and she wondered whether blueberries could be used as a dye. Her thoughts often turned to her knitting, and with it a keen sense of satisfaction.

The schoolteacher had the children sing a few songs for their visitors. Afterward she let them go to recess early and told Caleb how much help Rachel had been when she had apprenticed there. Rachel still had very little recollection of those days.

It was when they were walking home, Caleb holding her hand, the March wind blowing the last remnants of winter away, that she saw the curve in the road, and she remembered.

She stopped suddenly, pulling Caleb to a halt, since he was still holding her hand.

"What is it? Are you okay? What's wrong?"

"This is where it happened."

He didn't ask what she meant—instead he waited. He understood that this was a pivotal moment.

"I was walking home, a bit vexed that the school day hadn't gone well. I remember thinking I wasn't very *gut* at being a teacher, that I might never find what I was *gut* at."

She moved forward slowly, looked left and right, and then knelt down and touched a place on the ground where rocks were poking up through the soil.

"The car came around the corner so fast. One minute I was lost in thought, and the next I realized he was going to hit me. It was…blue—not a truck. I jumped out of the way at the same moment that he swerved, and I lost my balance. I remember thinking that I was going to stain my dress, and then nothing—nothing until I woke up in the family's van, unable to remember who I was or what I was doing there."

Her arms had begun to tremble. The memory was so strong that her heart raced as she recalled her fear and the throbbing in her head when she was in the van, and how nauseous she'd felt—how alone.

Caleb knelt beside her, put his arms around her and waited.

When she'd composed herself, she said, "It's a weight off me, to know…to have at least that memory back."

She didn't realize that she was crying until he reached forward and wiped away her tears.

"I'm not glad it happened to you, Rachel, but I am so very thankful that *Gotte* used it to bring us together."

They walked the rest of the way home in silence. When she turned toward the front porch, Caleb tugged on her hand and nodded toward the garden. So they went there, found her mother's bench and sat and watched the birds hop from bush to bush, searching for seeds.

"I need to tell you something." He waited until she turned her attention completely to him. "I love you, Rachel Yoder, and I want to marry you."

"You do?"

"I do. I've told you of my feelings many times, on Christmas Day, and in our letters."

"I was afraid you were having second thoughts."

"*Nein*. I'm sure of my feelings. It's only that…"

"Are you worried about my moods? About my condition?"

"I am not. You are perfect exactly as you are. Everyone struggles with something, Rachel. At least you are dealing with your situation."

"Am I not conservative enough for you?" Perhaps she shouldn't have gone on and on about her knitting business, about the yarns and dyes, about her hopes to sell in *Englisch* shops.

"You are perfect. Conservative or liberal doesn't matter so long as we share the same faith. We can work out our differences."

"Then what is it? I hear a *but* in your voice."

"I can't leave my parents. I can't leave them alone."

"And I wouldn't ask you to."

"This is what I am struggling with. I see how much better you are here. How can I take you from this place? Your family..."

"Is loud and complicated and exhausting, and I love them, but, Caleb, my family is my roots. They always will be." She looked down at their hands. It felt so natural for her hand to be cradled in his. "You? You are my future."

"Your *bruder* said as much."

"He did?"

"Ya." He shook his head. "At times it seems like my thinking is muddled. I'm unable to move forward or see a solution until someone points out the obvious."

"Ethan pointed out the obvious?"

"He told me if I was so worried about taking you from here, to go home and build you a sunroom."

"And you would do that for me?"

"Ya. That and so much more."

He pulled her into his arms then, held her in the warm afternoon sun. She breathed in the scent of him, the comfort of his presence, and she prayed that he would never let her go.

"You're so precious to me, Rachel. You brought color into my life."

"And you brought hope into mine."

"You made me look at things honestly, things I'd been too stubborn to see, but now…now I can see that our life is *gut*—our Plain life is *gut*, in all its variations."

"The future might not always be as bright and hopeful as today," she whispered. The old fear pushed against her hopes and dreams of happiness, but Caleb only laughed.

"We're both old enough to know that every life has its share of trouble, but we can face those days together. *Gotte* will see us through."

"He's certainly guided us through to this point, and who would have ever imagined the course our lives took."

Caleb kissed her again, pressed his forehead to hers and whispered, "And He can be trusted with our future, as well."

Which was a truth that Rachel understood better every day—she could feel it, ringing through her heart.

Epilogue

The wedding took place a short eight weeks later. Rachel had feared those eight weeks would drag by, but in fact they flew. There was so much to do, and she felt a lightness in her heart that she'd never known before.

They married in her parents' yard, under the tall oak tree. She wore a lavender dress with a matching lavender apron. Her *kapp* was brand-new. Family and friends and church members filled the benches that had been set up across the grass. Caleb's parents sat in the front row with her parents. The event would last all day and include lunch, dinner and games for the *youngies*. A long table on the front porch held the gifts that those attending had brought—dishes and sheets and towels and more than one quilt. They would be living with Caleb's parents at first, but Rachel knew the items would come in handy.

Although many Amish couples did not take honeymoons, they had opted to travel to Niagara Falls, a place she'd always longed to see. It helped that there was a large alpaca farm in the vicinity that they both had an interest in visiting.

Rachel was looking forward to the trip, but even more than that she was looking forward to returning to the quaint house in Montgomery, Indiana. Caleb had already begun work on a sunroom, for when the days turned dark. "Plus you'll need a place for your shop," he noted.

She planned to offer not only her sheep yarn and finished projects, but also alpaca yarn and Ida's crocheted items. Their days would be full and, hopefully, *Gotte* would bless them with many children.

Morning sunshine fell through the trees as she and Caleb stood in front of the bishop. Caleb looked terribly handsome in his black suit—a traditional Amish suit that appeared to be brand-new. It wasn't what he was wearing that pierced her heart, but the way he looked at her.

"Do you, Caleb Wittmer, and you, Rachel Yoder, vow to remain together until death?" Bishop Joel studied them both over his reading glasses. He wasn't old as bishops went—not nearly as old as Bishop Amos—and yet there was a quiet wisdom about him. He had been a calming, guiding presence in her life, especially since she'd returned home. She was suddenly grateful for him, and so glad that he was presiding over her wedding.

"We do."

"And will you both be loyal and care for each other during adversity?"

"We will."

"And during affliction?"

"Yes."

"And during sickness?"

Caleb squeezed her hands.

"We will."

Joel tucked his Bible under his arm and covered their hands with his own. "All of those assembled here, as your *frienden* and family in Christ, and I, as your bishop, wish you the blessing and mercy of *Gotte*."

There were shouts of "Amen" and "Praise *Gotte*" and even "Hallelujah." Rachel gazed up into Caleb's eyes and felt as if his love was showering over her, covering her, blessing her.

"Go forth in the Lord's name." Bishop Joel turned them to face their guests. "You are now man and wife."

Her *mamm* was crying. Miriam was trying to shift baby Stevie to her left arm and clap at the same time. Becca and Clara were practically hopping up and down, and Ethan and her *dat* looked proud enough to bust a button. Ida was crying and John had his arm around her.

They walked back down the aisle, through the gathering of family and friends, and Rachel knew that this was a day she'd never forget.

After the ceremony and before the luncheon, Caleb whispered into her ear, "Care for a walk in the garden?"

Which was exactly what she needed to hear.

Her mother's vegetables were knee-high, and the flowers were a sight to behold.

As soon as they turned the corner in the garden, Caleb pulled her into his arms.

"I love you, Rachel Yoder."

"Rachel Wittmer now."

"I love you, Rachel Wittmer."

And those words were all she needed to hear to make her day the perfect memory. Their first Christmas together would be one that she would always remember, as was their first meeting, when she didn't know who she was and Caleb hadn't a clue as to how to deal with a pushy, moody stranger. But her dreams and hopes and prayers were filled with their future together—future Christmases, possibly dark days and certainly days of joy. The stuff of life, and she was ready, finally, to embrace it.

* * * * *

If you loved this story,
pick up the first book in the
Indiana Amish Brides series

A Widow's Hope

from bestselling author
Vannetta Chapman

Available now from Love Inspired!

Find more great reads at www.LoveInspired.com

Dear Reader,

Our memories are dear to us—we keep pictures on our phones, frame schoolwork from our children and place our wedding photograph on the mantel. In many ways, our memories define us. When those memories are stripped away, we're left simply with who we have become. We're left with the knowledge that our Heavenly Father knows us—truly knows us—and cares for us more than we can fathom.

As Rachel rediscovers her past, she also learns to trust the woman she has become. And without that past, she must depend on the kindness of strangers. God provides for her, even in the midst of her pain and confusion. God is with her, even when she doesn't know exactly who or where she is.

Caleb is very busy with the life that he believes God has laid out before him. He scarcely has time for rescuing ladies in distress, or making new friends, or listening to his heart. Furthermore, he clings to tradition as if it were the single thing keeping him afloat on the sea of life. Then he meets Rachel, a quite untraditional person, and God begins to work on Caleb's heart and set into motion the special plans He has for him.

I hope you enjoyed reading *Amish Christmas Memories*. I welcome comments and letters at vannettachapman@gmail.com.

May we continue to "always give thanks to God the Father for everything, in the name of our Lord Jesus Christ" (*Ephesians* 5:20).

Blessings,

Vannetta

SPECIAL EXCERPT FROM

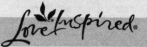

Pregnant and abandoned by her Englisher *boyfriend, Dori Bontrager returns home—but she's determined it'll be temporary. Can Eli Hochstetler convince her that staying by his side in their Amish community is just what she and her baby need?*

Read on for a sneak preview of
Courting Her Prodigal Heart *by Mary Davis, available January 2019 from Love Inspired!*

Rainbow Girl stepped into his field of vision from the kitchen area. *"Hallo."*

Eli's insides did funny things at the sight of her.

"Did you need something?"

He cleared his throat. "I came for a drink of water."

"Come on in." She pulled a glass out of the cupboard, filled it at the sink and handed it to him.

"Danki."

She gifted him with a smile. *"Bitte.* How's it going out there?"

He smiled back. "Fine." He gulped half the glass, then slowed down to sips. No sense rushing.

After a minute, she folded her arms. "Go ahead. Ask your question."

"What?"

"You obviously want to ask me something. What is it? Why do I color my hair all different colors? Why do I dress like this? Why did I leave? What is it?"

She posed all *gut* questions, but not the one he needed an answer to. A question that was no business of his to ask.

"Go ahead. Ask. I don't mind." Very un-Amish, but she'd offered. *Ne*, insisted.

He cleared his throat. "Are you going to stay?"

She stared for a moment, then looked away. Obviously not the question she'd expected, nor one she wanted to answer.

He'd made her uncomfortable. He never should have asked. What if she said *ne*? Did he want her to say *ja*? "You don't have to tell me." He didn't want to know anymore.

She pinned him with her steady brown gaze. "I don't know. I don't want to, but I'm sort of in a bind at the moment."

Maybe for the reason she'd been so sad the other day, which had made him feel sympathy for her.

He appreciated her honesty. "Then why does our bishop think you are?"

"He's hoping I do."

His heart tightened. "Why are you giving him false hope?" Why was she giving Eli false hope?

"I'm not. I've told him this is temporary. He won't listen. Maybe you could convince him to stop this foolishness—" she waved her hand toward where the building activity was going on "—before it's too late."

He chuckled. "You don't tell the bishop what to do. *He* tells you."

He really should head back outside to help the others. Instead, he filled his glass again and leaned against the counter. He studied her over the rim of his glass. Did he want Rainbow Girl to stay? She'd certainly turned things upside down around here. Turned him upside down. Instead of working in his forge—where he most enjoyed spending time—he was here, and gladly so. He preferred working with iron rather than wood, but today, carpentry strangely held more appeal.

Time to get back to work. He guzzled the rest of his water and set the glass in the sink. *"Danki."* As he turned to leave, something on the table caught his attention. The door knocker he'd made years ago for Dorcas—Rainbow Girl—ne, Dorcas, but now Rainbow Girl had it. They were the same person, but not the same. He crossed to the table and picked up his handiwork. "You kept this?"

She came up next to him. *"Ja.* I liked having a reminder of…"

"Of what?" Dare he hope him?

She stared at him. "Of…my life growing up here."

That was probably a better answer. He didn't need to be thinking of her as anything more than a lost *Englisher*.

Don't miss Courting Her Prodigal Heart *by Mary Davis, available January 2019 wherever Love Inspired® books and ebooks are sold.*

www.LoveInspired.com